THE Duelist's SEDUCTION
LAUREN SMITH

D1314676

This book is a work of fiction. Names, characters, places, and incidents are the product of the author's imagination or are used fictitiously. Any resemblance to actual events, locales, or persons, living or dead, is coincidental.

Copyright © 2015 by Lauren Smith
Edited by Theresa Cole
Excerpt from *Wicked Designs* by Lauren Smith
Excerpt from *Tempted by A Rogue* by Lauren Smith
Cover design by Fiona Jayde Media
Cover art by Fiona Jayde Illustrator

All rights reserved. In accordance with the U.S. Copyright Act of 1976, the scanning, uploading, and electronic sharing of any part of this book without the permission of the publisher constitutes unlawful piracy and theft of the author's intellectual property. If you would like to use material from the book (other than for review purposes), prior written permission must be obtained by contacting the publisher at ldsmith1818@gmail.com. Thank you for your support of the author's rights.

First ebook and print on demand edition as part of *Captivated By His Kiss* Collection: January 2015

Reprint as a single novella ebook edition: May 2015

The publisher is not responsible for websites (or their content) that are not owned by the publisher.

ISBN: 978-0-9962079-3-5

OTHER TITLES BY LAUREN SMITH

Historical
The League of Rogues Series
Wicked Designs
His Wicked Seduction
Her Wicked Proposal
Wicked Rivals (Coming Fall 2016)
The Seduction Series
The Duelist's Seduction
The Rakehell's Seduction (Coming soon)
The Rogue's Seduction (Coming soon)
Standalone Stories
Tempted by A Rogue

Contemporary
The Surrender Series
The Gilded Cuff
The Gilded Cage
The Gilded Chain
Her British Stepbrother
Forbidden: Her British Stepbrother
Seduction: Her British Stepbrother
Climax: Her British Stepbrother

Paranormal
Dark Seductions Series
The Shadows of Stormclyffe Hall
The Love Bites Series
The Bite of Winter
Brotherhood of the Blood Moon Series
Blood Moon on the Rise

DEDICATION

For Amanda who is always there to support me, and is the queen of story plotting sessions.

TABLE OF CONTENTS

Dear Readers,

I began my writing journey several years ago, a true "green girl" when it came to romance. *The Duelist's Seduction* was my first story, one that began my love affair with writing historical romances. In the following pages, you'll meet Gareth and Helen, the hero and heroine. Gareth is a stubborn man, hurting, wounded, and full of pride. Please forgive him for being so, he does change, I assure you. All great romances require the hero and heroine to change. So if he is a tad blunt, a little rude, a little cold, just know that he won't always be so. The way he and Helen meets is undeniably dark, and the circumstances certainly questionable, but if you can, fearless reader, stay with them, you might find their happily ever after is very sweet and satisfying. Helen, with her soft heart, is different from most heroines you expect to read about today, she is not weak in her spirit. She has a will to love against all odds. I hope you'll take a chance on Gareth and Helen and enjoy their story.

CHAPTER ONE

The predawn sky shone brightly with flickering stars as Helen Banks readied herself for the duel. Her hair was coiled and pinned tightly against her head, concealing its thick mass and giving her a boyish look—a disguise she prayed would last. Checking the black mask covering her face, she resumed walking. She took a deep, steadying breath as she adjusted her breeches and the black coat she'd pinched from her brother's wardrobe.

The open field near the spa city of Bath was quiet. Two coaches waited in the distance along the roadside, and ahead of her, two men waited, watching her approach. Not even a breeze dared rustle the knee-high grass as Helen walked up to her enemy and his second. Both men also wore masks to conceal their identities should someone witness the illegal duel. The paling skies played with the retreating shadows of night, lending a melancholy air to the moment she stopped inches from the men.

"You are late, Mr. Banks," the taller of the two men announced coldly.

With his broad shoulders and muscular body, Gareth Fairfax cut an imposing figure. He seemed perpetually tense, as though ready to strike out at anyone who might offend him. Dark hair framed his chiseled features, and the eyes that glowered from between the spaces of his mask were a fathomless blue. They were the sort of eyes a woman lost herself in, like gazing into a dark pool of water that seemed to sink endlessly, drawing her in until she can't find her way back to the surface. She recognized the sensual, full lips, now thinned by anger, and the gleam of his eyes on her. She was never more thankful that the early morning's pale light did not expose her as being a woman.

Helen hated knowing that even now, faced with possible death at his hands, she still desired him. Having seen him from afar over the past few months, she'd been enchanted. Gareth—for that was the way she'd dreamt about him, not as Mr. Fairfax—had a way about him, an animal magnetism that drew her in, with his smoky gaze and relaxed movements. Sin personified—she'd once heard a woman describe him thus at a dance and it was true. Even angels would be tempted to stray to hell for one glance, one lingering, seductive look. He smiled so rarely, she'd glimpsed it but twice in the months she'd seen him. Both times it had fairly knocked her off her feet with the sheer force of its power.

He'd never noticed her at the social engagements. She had stood close to the wall, quiet and lost in dreams as she watched him through her heavy lashes. Foolish, too, she knew, to look at him and feel such hunger for the things his brooding demeanor promised. He had passed her by on numerous occasions, but his head never turned and his eyes never alighted on her. Even now, as she stood before him, ready to die at his hands, she knew he thought her to be her twin brother, Martin.

If he ever discovered she was a woman, he would be appalled and furious. Especially given that she was only dueling him to save her brother's life.

She briefly studied her opponent's second. He was just as tall, his features nearly as striking as Gareth's.

Helen choked down a shaky breath. "I was waylaid." She prayed her voice sounded gruff and masculine.

Gareth's eyes were dark orbs, burning with thinly controlled anger. He shifted restlessly on his feet, his imposing form momentarily revealed by the dark blue coat that contoured to his shape.

"Is this your second?" His growl sent shivers down her spine as his glaze flicked to the squat man in his mid-thirties standing behind her. She glanced over her shoulder, widening her eyes in silent encouragement for her second to come closer.

"I am," Mr. Rodney Bennett replied and bowed.

"Mr. Banks, I am Mr. Ambrose Worthing,"

Gareth's second announced politely.

Well, finally someone was acting like a gentleman. "Mr. Worthing," Helen said, making sure to keep her voice low. "Allow me to introduce my second, Mr. Rodney Bennett."

Bennett passed by Helen, and he and Worthing shook hands. Bennett offered the pistols to Worthing for inspection. Since Gareth and Worthing had not brought the weapons, that duty fell to her as the challenged party. As the two men drew apart from her and Gareth, she tried not to stare at him. He was impossibly handsome, in that dark, mysterious sort of way that a woman simply couldn't ignore. Like gazing upon a visage of an angry god, all fire and might, ready to burn her to ash with passion.

Her opponent glowered at her. "I suppose I should trust that you've not tampered with my pistol?"

His icy tone made her bristle with indignation. "You have my word it shoots fair," Helen snapped. The nerve of the man to accuse her of cheating!

"Your word? We would not be here if I could trust your word. A man who does not honor his debts may not find it necessary to honor the rules of a duel," Gareth retorted.

She wanted to scream. Her fists clenched at her sides. Her nails dug painfully into her palms as she struggled to calm down. She wanted to throttle her brother, whose rash and inconsiderate behavior had gotten her into this mess.

"Easy, Fairfax. Both pistols appear to be in working order," Worthing announced as he and

Bennett rejoined them.

Helen breathed a sigh of relief as Bennett resumed his position behind her. She'd paid him the last bit of money she'd had for him to appear as her second. She didn't really know the man, having only met him briefly when she'd had to drag her brother away from the card tables a few nights ago. When she first approached Bennett with her plan, he had tried to talk her out of it, but when she offered money, he couldn't refuse and had agreed to help her take her brother's place in the duel. Even though he was a gentleman, the gambler inside him craved any bit of money he could get his hands on to return to the tables. She was lucky he hadn't gambled away his pair of pistols, or else she would have been completely humiliated to turn up at a duel without weapons.

"Now," Mr. Worthing said, "before we settle this, is it possible that you and Mr. Banks can reconcile the dispute?"

Helen started to nod, wanting desperately to find a way to settle the problem without bloodshed, but Gareth spoke up, stilling the bobbing of her head.

"Mr. Banks has run up a debt to me of over a thousand pounds. He has not been able to pay it back to me over the last three months. Furthermore, he created an additional liability of five hundred pounds last evening when he played with money he did not have."

Helen swallowed hard, a painful lump in her throat choking her. *Martin, you damned fool…*

"Why did you accept his vouchers then?" Rodney spoke up. "I saw you agree to play with him. You didn't have to."

"Banks had money on him. I assumed he'd replenished his funds and would settle his debts to me." Gareth shot a withering look in Helen's direction. "Shooting him will be a bonus."

Helen held his stare for a moment, feeling the regret deep in her belly that she hadn't known better than to trust her twin brother—too childish for a gentleman of one-and-twenty—to be more responsible. Instead of helping to secure her a position as a governess—their finances dim after the death of their parents and no good marriages likely—he had been losing what meager fortune they had to men like Gareth Fairfax, who had plenty to spare.

A man who would now take her life as payment for a debt she didn't owe. But what else could she do? She couldn't let Martin die. A man had options to survive, a woman did not, at least not one that wouldn't make her despise herself for the rest of her life.

Her memory of the previous night was tinged with fury and disappointment in Martin. Her heart had plummeted into the pit of her stomach when she'd retired for the evening and found his room empty. All of her hopes were dashed the moment she'd learned he'd gone back to the gambling tables.

She'd hidden in the shadows outside the gambling hell, trying not to be seen by anyone passing by. The smell of alcohol stung her nose, and the raucous laughter echoing from the entrance sent chills of trepidation down her spine. It would ruin her completely if she were witnessed outside such an establishment. Bennett had promised to bring Martin out to her, but when Martin emerged, he was being roughly hauled out by a dark-haired gentleman, a man she recognized, a man she'd admired for the last few months from afar.

"I'll honor my debt to you, Mr. Fairfax," Martin had drunkenly promised, over and over again.

Gareth Fairfax, following behind her brother, grabbed Martin by his coat collar and rammed him up against the stone wall of the nearest building.

"Honor your debt? With what, pray tell? You played that last hand without a shilling to your name," Gareth growled. "You haven't even redeemed your vowels for the last few times of play. I demand satisfaction." Gareth released Martin, who sagged against the wall in defeat.

Martin's head had bowed wearily in submission. "Name the location and time."

"There is a field two miles east of the Crow tavern. Be there tomorrow morning one hour before the sun rises. There is a full moon. That will do. I have no intention of being chased out of the country because of you. Bring a second and your choice of weapon." Gareth had stalked off, leaving Martin alone. He shook his head as though to clear it, and with steps none too steady, started walking in Helen's direction.

When he passed by the alcove where she was hiding, she stepped out and struck her brother as hard as she could on the shoulder. Her anger flared. "You fool! That man is going to kill you!"

"Helen?" Martin said in shock. "What the bloody

hell are you doing here? You should be at home."

She narrowed her eyes. "I had hoped to get you out of that place before you lost everything we have. It seems I am too late." She hoped her accusation stung. It was nothing less than he deserved.

Martin glanced at her. Under the glow of the streetlight, she saw guilt deepening the color of his lightly tanned skin.

"I'm sorry, Helen… I thought I could win back our money and more." His tone was apologetic, but it lost some of its effect when he hiccupped.

Helen waited for Martin to say something, but he did not. Her voice shook with a mixture of fear and fury. "I forbid you to go tomorrow morning. What will I do if you die, Martin?"

"I won't die," he replied sullenly. "I'm a crack shot. I stand an even chance."

"An even chance of what?" Helen nearly shrieked. "Killing a man and being made to leave the country? Do you even care what would happen to me without you?"

"Is that all I am? Someone to take care of you?" he shot back.

Helen's eyes burned with tears and she threw her arms around her brother. "No, you fool. I love you. I don't want to lose you. How can you not understand that? After mama and papa…" her voice broke, but she forced herself to continue. "I *cannot* lose you, too."

"Well it doesn't matter, does it? I have to meet Fairfax tomorrow." Her brother's mouth assumed a mulish cast, and she knew it would do no good to argue with him.

He was as stubborn as their father had been. They did not speak the rest of the way back to their lodgings, but Helen's mind worked frantically. She loved Martin, he was her other half, as any true twins were. She had to save him, had to find a way to fix what he'd done, or if not fix it, then sacrifice herself for him. It was the only way. One of them had to survive, and he stood a better chance on his own than she did.

She'd formed a plan. She and her brother were almost the same height, and their build was similar enough that as children they'd often been mistaken for one another. If she dressed as a male, could she pass for him? When her brother woke up early the next morning to prepare for the duel, Helen took her father's cane, one of the last pieces of his belongings they hadn't sold, and knocked Martin out. She dressed in an extra set of his clothes and locked Martin in his room.

It was a simple solution to a complex problem. Martin was a man and could live on without her. It was easier for men to make their way in the world. A penniless young lady with no family and no connections had no such luck. The best she could hope for was a position as a governess or companion, and without references, those positions were almost impossible to find. The only other possibility was one she would not consider. Even being a maid would be better than selling her body.

And that was how she'd ended up on this field,

facing the one man she'd dreamt about dancing with and knowing she never would. A man above her in station, money, and power. A man with secretive smiles, and a soft, low seductive voice, surrounded by rumors whispered behind fans in the assembly halls of how he must make a good lover. She would never know if any of it was true now, not that she'd ever had a chance to earn his interest at the balls before.

Mr. Worthing cleared his throat. "Fairfax, would you be willing to work with Mr. Banks?"

Even in the pre-dawn light, Helen could see Gareth's face darken in anger. "I would find a way to repay you, sir," Helen said quickly. Like a man about to be hanged, she clung to the last few minutes she'd have of life, even if it meant lying. There would be no way to repay him, of course, but she had to try. She had to hope her opponent still had some kindness and would delay her demise a few precious seconds.

"You've had weeks to repay me, and I've not seen one shilling. There will be no settlement." Gareth's tone was quieter, almost resigned, as he checked his pistol, flicked his glance at her, and then nodded to Worthing.

So much for compassion. The last hope of her survival had died with his curt nod. Helen's heart kicked into a faster pace. Her fear created a bitter, metallic taste in her mouth as she realized she'd been hoping the duel wouldn't actually happen. But of course it would. Men like Gareth valued honor, and her brother had none. This duel was unavoidable.

Worthing sighed heavily, apparently convinced there was no turning back. He and Bennett walked several yards away to watch the proceedings.

She and Gareth were alone, closer than they'd ever been before tonight. How many times had she peered through the crowds of dancers in the assembly rooms and watched him dance with other women, wishing she was the one that close to him? Now here she was, close enough to dance, but it was to be a dance of death. A hollow ache filled her chest at the thought, and a whisper of fear made her heart shudder behind her ribs.

I don't want to die, but what choice is there?

The faint breeze brought his scent of sandalwood and the faintest hint of horses and leather to her nose. The aroma made her homesick for the stables in her parents' home in the country, a home she and Martin had to sell in order to survive. The pistol grew heavier in her hands, the wood and metal sinking into her palm with force as she curled her fingers around it more securely. The silence and her fear made it all suddenly unbearable.

"Very well," Helen growled, losing her ability to remain calm and still any longer. The only way to quell her fear was to embrace her anger. "Name your distance, sir." If she was to die, let it be done already. This waiting and delay was eating away at her courage.

"Thirty paces." Gareth replied after a moment's hesitation. He seemed to be peering at her more sharply, as though something had attracted his attention. His usually sensual full lips were thinned into a frown. Surely he couldn't have realized she wasn't Martin... She had to distract him.

"Thirty." She nodded, relieved to know it helped

mask the way her entire body shook with a new wave of fear. She'd never imagined facing death like this, especially not at the hands of a man she desired. Fate was cruel. "Let us finish this." She turned her back to Gareth and waited.

He closed the distance between them and put his back up against hers. She shivered at the sudden warmth of his body against hers, his backside pressed ever so lightly against her lower back. His clothing whispered against hers, like a strange sort of dance, and then Gareth moved away as Mr. Worthing began to count. She began to mark the paces as well, trying to ignore the roaring of blood in her ears and the realization that each step brought her that much closer to her death.

When Mr. Worthing called out to halt Helen and Gareth at thirty paces, they turned to face each other. The velvet skies were paler now, as though the stars had blinked, closing their celestial eyes to miss the grisly scene about to unfold below. Helen saw Gareth turn sideways and raise his arm. She copied the movement, aiming her pistol at Gareth's chest. The pale moonlight glinted off the gun in his hand as he trained it on her chest. Her entire body started to shake as instinctive fear took over. There was a pistol pointed at her heart. Her hand trembled, the barrel of her own gun wavering. She wouldn't shoot him, there was no doubt of that.

"One," Worthing called out. "Two…"

Helen's eyes shot up from Gareth's pistol to his face. He was far enough away to appear more a shadow dressed in black with glowing eyes than the man she'd longed to share the secrets of her heart with.

"Three—"

Her finger clenched around the trigger and she fired without meaning to. Her shot went wide, grazing Gareth's shoulder. He flinched but did not fire. Blood sprayed along his shirt, nearly black in the distance. She gasped and sucked in a violent breath, her vision spinning momentarily.

Horrified she had actually hit him, she dropped her pistol and it landed with a *thunk* in the grass. She ran over to him, reaching out to check the damage.

His dark eyes flashed in surprise as she clutched his arm and examined the wound.

"Oh Good Heavens!" she cried. "The one time I fire one of these stupid things..."

By the time she realized her higher feminine tone had betrayed her, Gareth, in one swift motion, had dropped his own pistol and grabbed her by the arm, dragging her against him. He ripped the mask from her face. Her pins sprung loose from the rough movement, releasing the bound up hair. The loose waves dropped down against her shoulders, the soft strands caressing her cheeks as she ducked her head, hiding her face from him. Gareth's look of rage turned to sheer astonishment.

"Where is Martin Banks?" His voice was rough and low. "And who the devil are you?"

His grip was too strong and Helen started to lose feeling in her arm. "Please, you're hurting me," she gasped.

Her plea went ignored. He didn't release his hold on her, but he lightened his hold so it was no longer bruising.

"Where is Banks?" He shook her and shouted angrily.

"Unconscious, in our lodgings." Helen tried to break free, but his iron grip held her fast. "I could not let you kill him." His eyes sharpened at her defiance.

Worthing and Bennett ran towards them.

"A woman?" Worthing called out in surprise. "Really, Fairfax...you should have told me," When Worthing strode over to her and Gareth, his eyes shifted between them as they stood locked together by Gareth's vice-like grip.

"Let go of her, Fairfax," Worthing slowly reached out and pried her loose from Gareth's arms.

Gareth batted Worthing's protective arm aside and gripped her by the shoulders, rattling her. "Who are you?" he snarled, his white, even teeth shining in the dim light. "Why are you here in Banks's place?"

"Let go of her," Bennett growled and moved a step toward Gareth. Worthing lifted a hand to stay Bennett and tried once more to intervene, but Gareth dragged her away from Worthing's reach.

"Well? Answer me! I have no intention of hurting you, but I will get answers." His angry gaze bore into her like a hot poker.

Helen bit back furious tears. "I'm his sister. He is my only family." Her body started that awful shaking again, this time from the shock of being alive and unhurt. "I would be utterly alone should he perish."

"Don't you dare cry. I'll not be moved by a woman's tears," he threatened, but his grip softened immediately, belaying whatever cruelty hung in his words.

"Fairfax," Worthing cautioned at the same time Bennett said, "Release her!"

Everything happened so fast, it was almost a blur. Bennett tried to step between Gareth and Helen but stumbled back as Gareth pummeled him in the stomach. Helen screamed and struck out at Gareth, slapping him hard across the face. Worthing dove out of the way as Gareth tackled Helen to the ground. Bennett tried once more to rescue her but was felled by another punch from Gareth.

"Damnit Fairfax, hold off!" Worthing knelt by the unconscious Bennett.

"Keep that bloody fool away from me. I'm not going to hurt her," Gareth growled. "I want her to answer me." He was gazing down at her, a new light in his eyes, a light that was less dangerous, or perhaps more so, but in a different way. As though he was appraising her, or assessing her value, the way a man studies a good piece of horseflesh at the market when selecting a ride. It was not the gaze of a man who would strike out at her or wound her.

Helen gasped, struggling beneath Gareth's body. She wasn't afraid now, but more angry at the way he had manhandled her. He sat back on his heels, his knees on either side of her hips, still pinning her to the ground. His chest heaved with panting breaths, and his palms fell to his thighs.

She attempted to raise her hips but couldn't

budge. "Please, let me go." He tensed at her movement, his fingers digging into his thighs.

"Whatever shall I do with you, Miss Banks?" Gareth's breath evened out. "We have ourselves quite the problem."

"Fairfax…" Worthing's tone held an edge of warning. Gareth ignored him, a calculating gleam in his eyes.

Swallowing hard, she met his gaze as evenly as she could.

"I have a proposal for you, Miss Banks," Gareth said peacefully, but the shadows in his gaze made her wary. One of his hands drifted to her hair, allowing her blonde curls to cascade around and through his fingers. He suddenly smiled, taking one lock and twining it around his index finger, his eyes meeting hers. "If you come to my home with me, I will forget the debts owed to me. Or I send you back to Bath, find that scoundrel you call a brother, and finish this duel properly."

Helen blinked. Go home with Gareth Fairfax? She may have been an innocent, but she knew that if he were to take her to his home, she would be compromised—ruined for marriage. *Certainly ruined for any other man.* A blush warmed her whole body just thinking of what he would do to her if she agreed. *Ruined.* Part of her was filled with a secret, dark curiosity. Would he seduce her? She should have been more frightened by the fact that she was curious enough to wonder what it would be like to be with him. Women seemed to like seduction under the right circumstances. A spark of heat shot through her body at the thought of Gareth willfully seducing her.

"If I agree to go with you, what would you do with me?" The words came out thick, her tongue seemingly unable to form the words as she dared to ask about his intentions.

He didn't speak for a long moment. Instead he rubbed his thumb and forefinger against the lock of her hair. Finally, he let the loose curl drop and settled his hand back on his thigh, shifting his hips slightly. It pressed him harder against her and her own body flashed with a strange, queer sort of fire.

"You can settle your brother's debts to me one way or another." His tone was black as midnight, dark as sin, and rather than frighten her, it made her tremble with longing. She had heard enough women speak behind closed doors at the balls to know that what could happen between a man and woman in bed could be pleasurable for both parties.

Worthing stood up and eyed his friend. "Fairfax, you can't just take her home."

Gareth's eyes searched her face and settled on her lips. "She's already said that Banks is her only relative, Worthing. No one will miss her. It's her choice. She's free to leave, or she can come with me and save her brother's life."

"You can't be serious. The young woman was only defending her brother. You cannot ruin a lady over that."

She watched the exchange, wondering why Worthing was so ready to defend her.

"Well, Miss Banks?" He continued to study her,

his body keeping hers trapped as though there really was no option but to accept him. "Make your choice. Dawn is chasing us, and I, for one, don't wish to be here when the sun fully rises." He leaned down and whispered in her ear. "I promise to take good care of you and give you so much pleasure you might feel you'll die from it." The feel of his warm breath against the sensitive shell of her ear sent sparks shooting down her spine and she tensed.

Helen gazed up at him, desire running riotously through her body, and her mind whispered dark suggestions, borne of long years of need for things she barely understood. This was a chance to taste temptation, to be with a handsome man and know passion. There would never be love, she knew that, but passion might prove a memory worth having, especially with a man like him. Did she dare, though? Any chance of marrying, having children, would be at an end, and if anyone discovered where she was, her reputation would be ruined. Even obtaining employment as a maid would become difficult. Yet Martin would be safe, and he may yet find a way to make a living and support himself and her. It was a feeble hope, but that would be the only future she could hope for. Gareth had said he'd treat her well. Really, what choice did she have?

"Yes, Mr. Fairfax. I'll go with you."

The finality behind her words was heavy, and Gareth tensed above her, eyes widening. He hadn't expected her to agree? A ripple of power flowed through her. She liked surprising him. He scanned her face again, his eyes darkening, but not with anger.

This time it was something else that gleamed in their depths.

Worthing moved towards them, one hand raised. "Now, hold on Fairfax. I must insist you think this through."

Gareth slid off Helen and grabbed her arms, pulling her onto her feet. She barely heard the men arguing. All she was aware of was Gareth's hands on her body as he lifted her up and into him, letting her lean against his arm, as though aware she needed help to stand. The muscles beneath his shirt were taut and large. Heat emanated against her palms when she rested them briefly against his chest as she finally pushed away to stand on her own. He kept hold of her wrists, though, despite the tentative tug she gave to be released.

"I'm not in the mood for a lecture, Worthing. You take care of that…fellow. I will bring Miss Banks to my house. After you've seen to him, you can come and rescue the woman if you feel you must." There was a mixture of amusement and warning in Gareth's tone that confused Helen. "Provided you can convince her to go."

She tugged at her wrists, still trapped by his hands. Even though she'd agreed to accompany him, the fact that he still held her caused an unsettling heat to stir between her thighs. Helen clenched her legs together, desperate to stop the sensation. She tugged her hands again.

"Stop that," he growled and started walking.

Helen obeyed instantly. He was too strong for her to resist, so she followed, struggling to keep pace with his long-legged strides. They crossed the field and moved in the direction of the road where Helen had been dropped off by the hired conveyance. Gareth's coach stood waiting. The driver jumped down to lower the steps, and Gareth pulled her against him as he lifted her into the vehicle. Once they were settled inside, sharing the same seat, he shouted an order to the driver and the coach jerked forward. She rubbed her wrists, wondering if they'd bruise, and tried not to look at him. She failed.

He turned his head towards the window and away from her, his expression cool and unemotional. She couldn't believe that he actually desired her. Not when he'd had his pick of women in Bath. Compared to those other ladies, Helen knew she didn't measure up, so Gareth's choice made little sense.

"Why did you want me to come with you?" Helen dared herself to ask when the silence had stretched too long between them.

He fixed his cold gaze on her once more. "Because your brother must learn that his actions have consequences. If I have you, it will cause trouble for him. He'll have to find a way to marry you off after I'm done, not an easy task for a man with a ruined sister. It won't amount to the money he won off me, but it will be some measure of revenge."

Helen shut her eyes for a few minutes, jostled by the battering of the coach wheels on the rough road. Her stomach roiled with nausea. So he didn't desire her. Using her was only about revenge. Disappointment weighed her shoulders down, pressing on her chest. She sucked in a much needed breath. It was a cruel sort of feeling to go from believing she was desired to learning her seduction and ruination were merely payback for her brother's carelessness. In that moment, Helen felt very small and alone, uncared for, and unloved in the worst way. The most awful part was the way it seemed to take the wind from her sails. All of her high spirits, even the angry ones, were dashed upon the rocks. Would it be worth it—going with him, exploring her own passions—even when he might not feel them in return? There seemed no ready answer.

When she opened her eyes, he was staring at her still. This time, his eyes were more curious than cold. He had a beautiful profile—strong and straight like the statue of Michelangelo's David. How many hours at the balls and soirees had she spent studying each feature of him? Too many. As a wallflower, she'd had endless hours to memorize him, fantasize about him. What would she have said if only he'd asked her to dance once? A girlish dream, one that now lay dead in the field they'd just left. She would never be that woman, the one that handsome men would ask to dance or pay court to. She was just another woman who would go without love, and now, without marriage. Still, his face would haunt her forever. She could recall each line, each shape of his features... draw them perfectly from her dreams, if needed.

"What is your given name?" His question drew her from her thoughts.

"Helen," she replied, her eyes drawn to the curve of his lips as he smiled.

"Like fair Helen of Troy...do you bring ruin to

my kingdom?" he mused, more to himself than to her.

"I only wished to save my brother's life. Had I died, he would be no worse off than before. But had our positions been reversed… I would have no one to protect me."

"A tragedy to any woman," Gareth agreed.

At least he understood. She had no money and no friends. Without her brother, she'd be lost to decent society. She might have to sell herself to survive. Helen's lips quivered at that thought—to be so desperate for food that she would… A dark thought trespassed in her mind. Was agreeing to Gareth's proposal any better? She shivered at where such ideas led.

"Calm yourself." There was an underlying callousness to his words that rekindled her fire. "I'll not hurt you. No woman has ever left my bed with any complaints." His tone was layered with smug satisfaction. He leaned back in the coach seat, stretching out long, muscled legs, and crossing his boots at the ankles. She was reminded of a tomcat merely biding his time to make his move on the unsuspecting female cat he planned to mate with. She was the female cat in this scenario, and it did not make her feel safe at all. What little she'd heard of him from other ladies in society was that he wasn't rumored to be a cruel man. That was her only solace —that he wouldn't truly harm her.

The ride was long. Helen couldn't help but wonder what type of house he had, to live so far from Bath. At some point, fatigue overcame her. She didn't want to show weakness in front of him, but when her eyelids kept falling shut, she knew she was lost. Her head fell against Gareth's shoulder as she drifted off to sleep. She woke a while later when the pattern of the horses' hooves changed and the wheels slowed to a halt. Still drowsy, she raised her head from his shoulder, blushed when she realized he was staring at her, and scooted a little ways away. Running her hands through her hair, she tried to tame the wild waves.

Gareth opened the coach door and helped her out. He kept a gentle but firm grip on her arm as they walked up a set of stone steps. A matronly woman with graying hair waited for them just inside the door.

"Good, evening, Mary. Prepare a room for Miss Banks. She will be our guest for a time," Gareth said to the woman.

Mary's eyes widened in surprise, but she did not question him.

Helen gulped. How long was her stay to be? Gareth had not given any indication of its duration.

"Mr. Fairfax, how long do you intend to keep me here?" She held her breath so long her lungs burned.

He did not look at her as they followed Mary. "As long as necessary. I'll likely tire of you in a few weeks."

His words were a slap to her soul and she flinched.

Mary departed, winding her way up the grand staircase to prepare a room for her. Helen was once more alone with the brooding and frightening Gareth

Fairfax. He still held her arm as he escorted her to a mahogany and wine colored drawing room where a warm fire was lit. A pair of deep-backed chairs faced the fire, and Helen was pushed toward the one furthest from the door. Gareth took the other, his chair slightly angled toward her.

The dimness of the room, lit by only a few candles, and the roaring fire's warmth was seductive and inviting, like a strange sort of dream. Perhaps she was dreaming, and none of this was real. She'd wake soon and prepare a meager breakfast for Martin and…but she knew the truth. This was all too real and she was very vulnerable. A little tremor stole through her arms and chest.

"You find yourself in an unfortunate predicament, Miss Banks. I owe your brother a bullet. The duel was not finished. I've taken you, by your choice, in his place." His eyes reflected the fire's glow, wild and untamable.

Helen could not respond. Fascination rippled through her as she studied his lips, his eyes, his dark hair that gleamed in the firelight. He was a devil, but a handsome one, and his harsh gaze made her heart beat rapidly. It was madness to long for his seduction, to pray for it with every breath. Surely the fires of hell awaited her for her thoughts.

"My temper has cooled. I have no interest in shooting anyone at the moment, but your brother owes me a great deal of money." She'd expected him to be more businesslike, but there was a pensive musing to his voice that drew her in…made her wonder what he was truly thinking.

He seemed to be watching her for some reaction, but Helen did not understand the weight his words carried.

"We have no way of repaying you," she replied gravely. "I used the last bit of money I had to secure Mr. Bennett's support for the duel. I had hoped to gain a position as governess...that is, before Martin quarreled with you. If you give me time, I'm sure I could think of a way to settle our debt."

"Would you deny me, should I demand a different form of payment? It is why I brought you here, after all." The question was delivered very slowly and deliberately. His gaze raked up and down her body more savagely than she thought a look ever could. Helen paled, her earlier suspicion had been right.

"What would you have me do while I'm here?" Her words came out a strangled whisper. She knew what he would say, hoped breathlessly that he would, as dangerous and foolish as it was to wish for him to desire her.

Gareth stood up and, in one elegant move, came around behind her chair, his hands falling lightly onto her shoulders. He slowly swept her long hair away from her neck, baring part of her throat. One of his fingers drew a lazy pattern on her skin, teasing the tiny hairs which rose at his touch, and she shivered. He bent over the back of the chair, his lips brushing her ear as he spoke, stirring her senses.

"Remain here, at my beck and call, as a companion of sorts." He caught her chin with his hand and gently turned her face towards his, his lips so close to hers she could almost feel them. She swallowed uncomfortably as her mouth grew dry. "When I tire of you, I shall return you to Bath, and your brother's debt will be fully paid." His hands slid down her shoulders, along the sides of her arms. For the first time in her life, she was torn, her mind and heart were warning her against him, but her body was enticed by the slightest touch of his hands, the brush of his lips. Her face flushed with heat as he kissed her softly below the ear.

"And if I refuse?" The room slowly spun, and her head filled with a strange buzzing. Her skin tingled beneath his touch. She ought to refuse. Staying here would ruin her respectability…the last thing she had left that couldn't be bought or destroyed, except it seemed, by this dark, brooding man. Yet she'd chosen, as he'd reminded her, to come here voluntarily. She couldn't lie to herself. She'd known of his intentions to bed her from the start, but she longed to test him, to see what he would say if she pretended to change her mind.

"Then I lock you in a room here and ride straight to Bath to find your brother." Gareth's words were sinister, but his voice was as smooth as honey. Helen's eyelashes fluttered down against her cheeks as she fought to hide her emotions. It wouldn't be wise for him to know his power over her…how easily he enthralled her with the carnal promise in his eyes. He came back around to stand in front of her.

"So, Miss Banks, will you accept?" He crossed his arms in front of his chest, looking down at her imperiously.

Helen rose from her chair, glad for her height. She needed to be his equal if she was going to accept this bargain. He didn't tower over her as much as he would have other women. For a long moment, she gazed back at him, weighing her options. Ruin herself and save her brother? Or save herself and sign her brother's death sentence. Sadly, the choice was easier than it ought to have been. She would do *anything* to protect Martin. And she'd also not refuse herself this one chance to know passion.

"I accept, so long as you vow that my brother will not be harmed and his debt to you will be satisfied." Her voice didn't waver.

Gareth nodded slowly. "I will honor those terms."

Helen held out a hand to shake upon it. "Then we have a bargain."

Gareth looked down at her hand, a slow smile spreading across his lips. He took her hand and before she could protest, he tugged her into his arms. It was her first kiss, and not at all what she had expected. This was no innocent meeting of lovers' lips. Gareth's mouth caught hers, moving in deep, teasing motions that sent shivers down her spine. One of his hands coiled in her hair, twining his fingers in her silky strands. He clenched, just enough to cause her to open her mouth wider in a gasp born of pleasure at the slight pain. He plundered her mouth, his tongue diving to mate with hers.

A throbbing pulse burst into life between her legs and her knees gave way, knocking against his. He wound an arm about her waist, holding her to him.

Like a limp ragdoll, she surrendered to his amorous attentions, the sensations overwhelming and intoxicating. She wished she knew what to do—how to move her lips, where to place her hands—to please him in return.

His hand in her hair held her captive for his exploring mouth, which tasted her lips, her neck, her collarbone, and behind her ears. And then it was over. He spun her gently out of his grasp, grinning at her smugly.

"That is how we seal our bargain, my darling."

The glare she sent him only made him smile.

He gestured for her to follow him. "I'm sure Mary has prepared your chamber by now." Helen trailed behind him as they left the drawing room. An upstairs maid stood at the foot of the stairs, waiting.

"The lady's room is ready, sir," the ginger-haired maid bobbed in a shallow curtsey.

"Thank you, Mira. Which room is it?"

"The third guest room on the right, sir." The maid looked expectantly to Gareth.

"That will be all, Mira. Run along to bed."

Helen watched as the maid ducked back down the stairs and through a door that probably led to the servants' quarters. It took every ounce of her will not to call out for the maid to stay and not leave them alone. She wasn't afraid of him, but nerves made her shaky. There was so much about being with a man in bed that she didn't know. Any woman with good sense would be nervous about her first time, even though he'd assured her she would enjoy it. Gareth tugged Helen's hand, forcing her to follow him up the stairs and down the hall. He paused at the third room on the right, just as the maid had directed. The door stood open, the room ready for her.

It had a beautiful four-poster bed with velvet hangings and a ruby red coverlet. A thin white nightgown lay draped over the middle of the bed. Walking away from him, Helen picked the garment up, admiring its beautiful but simple design. She had never owned anything so fine in her life. Rather than bid her goodnight, Gareth came into the room and shut the door. The snick of the door settling into the frame held a frightening finality. They were alone again. Helen backed away in fear, her heart racing. Did he mean to take her so soon?

I am not ready. I want him, but I am not prepared.

Gareth walked over to the armoire that faced the bed and tapped it lightly.

"There are gowns in here. They may not fit properly, but I will have my housekeeper send for ones that will. You may rest a while if you wish. Mary will be here to help you dress later in the morning. It has been some time since you've eaten, I assume. The servants will prepare whatever you wish after you've rested." He came back to her, cupping her chin, his voice gentler than it had been since they'd first met on the field for the duel.

"Th...thank you, Mr. Fairfax," Helen stammered, her body shaking slightly with fear.

She'd had such courage in the field, ready to face death for her brother, but this was so different. She'd come here, agreeing to be his mistress, in a fashion.

She had little knowledge of the ways of men. Would he prepare her for their joining? Or would he be ruthless, take her hard, and not think a moment about her pleasure? The second the thought passed her mind, she shoved it aside. Helen had made a study of Gareth over the last few months, seen him interact with men and women, and she knew enough of reading a person's character to know he wouldn't hurt her. But he also wouldn't let her walk away from what she'd promised to give him.

"Mr. Fairfax—" she stammered.

"I give you leave to address me by my Christian name, Gareth." He smiled again, his eyes shining with hidden laughter. "You're afraid of me." He teased.

Helen clasped her shaking hands together. "Of course I am. You were going to shoot me. And now I'm here…unchaperoned in your house with the agreement between us that I share your bed. I've never been with a man, and frankly, the prospect of it scares me a little. I would be a fool to not be a little afraid."

"You certainly are no fool. Feisty, but not foolish. A unique trait in a woman. You've no reason to fear me. There will be only pleasure between us." Gareth slowly reached out and captured her hips, his fingers digging for a better hold as he drew her against him. The smile that curved his lips heated her blood and sent her heart skittering. He rocked her into him, as though he meant to give her a gentle, teasing shake to cheer her up and relax her.

"Prepare yourself, Helen. I am going to kiss you again." And he did. A feathery brush of lips on lips. Helen's eyes drifted shut at the pleasurable sensation of his embrace.

The kiss changed, becoming slow and deep, his tongue easing between her lips. The sensation was strange, but Helen found herself kissing him back, her own tongue exploring him in turn. She was barely aware of him pushing her back against the bedpost until the wood dug between her shoulder blades. Gasping against him, she shuddered as he unbuttoned her breeches and slid his palm down her abdomen to part the thatch of pale curls between her legs. Gareth pinned her body with his, trapping her against the bedpost while using his hand to cup her mound. She tensed, gasping as he rubbed her with the heel of his hand. The rough pad of his thumb brushed her sensitive bud while another figure probed at the throbbing folds. She bit her lip, whimpering at the powerful zing of pleasure from his touch, and her body bucked forward. Was this how it really felt to be with a man? To feel the riotous waves of building excitement? She wanted more, so much more.

"Please!" Helen could barely form a coherent thought. His thumb tweaked her again, stronger this time, and a second finger joined the first, pushing deep into her tight sheath.

"You like this?" Gareth growled against her neck, taking tiny tastes of her skin as he slid his fingers in and out, thrusting in a slow, deliberate pattern designed to drive her mad.

Her answer was a plaintive moan. She wrapped her arms around his neck, clinging to him for support.

"Soon, I will taste you here," he pressed firmly on

the bud, and the lightning flash of that touch exploded like a fire inside her.

"And I will take you here, hard and fast. Then so slow you will beg for mercy. And just when you drift off to sleep, I'll cover you again and thrust my cock so deep into you that you'll scream for more." As he spoke, his words were rough against her neck, tickling her skin, which was still damp from his kisses.

Helen gasped in breathless wonder as a powerful sensation spread through her, tingles, fire, and sparks alternating beneath her skin. Her knees knocked together as her legs gave out. His arms around her were the only thing keeping her upright. Gareth cupped her mound hard, holding her up as he continued to kiss her. She barely responded, too relaxed from the pleasure weighting her body with lethargy, so she merely consented to his rich plundering tongue. The fingers in her sheath withdrew, leaving her feeling strangely empty. But he moved his hand to her bottom, patting it softly as though to reward her for her inability to walk or talk. She knew she ought to have been indignant at his treatment of her, but she was too elated and drunk on the aftershocks of the explosion of sated desire which flashed and burned between her thighs.

He broke away when she started to seek his lips for another kiss. With a smirk of satisfaction, he left her alone in her bedchamber. She heard a click as something turned in the door. He had locked her in! She had agreed to stay here, but the sound of that lock turning infuriated her. She stumbled on weak legs to the door, tugging fiercely at the handle, which did not budge.

"Please… Gareth, let me out!" she called. "I said I would stay! Please!"

Silence.

He wanted her locked away. Why? Did he lie to her? Was he going to return to Bath, kill her brother, and return to take her to his bed? Surely, he couldn't be so cruel. Helen twisted at the knob again, hating that it didn't open, didn't budge an inch. She turned to look about the room. The thick paned windows weren't the type to open, and she wouldn't be able to break through it fast enough to escape without waking the entire house with the noise.

Helen choked down a panicked sob and abandoned the door. She prayed with every bit of her heart that Gareth hadn't decided to return to Bath and kill Martin. Maybe he had another reason for locking her in, even if she couldn't fathom why.

"Gareth, please…" she whispered into the wood of the door. Still silence. A wave of exhaustion swept her with such force that her head was too thick with a fog that made it hard to think. Gareth wouldn't kill Martin. He'd made a promise to her. Tomorrow she would demand to know why he'd locked her away tonight, and she would not let him do it again.

She retrieved the nightgown and, after a moment, prepared for bed. When she climbed between the sheets, she buried her face in the soft mound of pillows. Hot tears leaked from the corner of her eyes, soaking the cloth. Helen fought off the drowning despair that swamped her, but she couldn't hold long. Between this morning's near disaster on the field and the way Gareth had so coldly abandoned her just now, she was completely confused, both mentally and physically, and her crying grew harsh and ragged.

What had she done? She was trapped here by her own foolishness. And Martin... Would he try to find her? Would Gareth kill him if he came here? It was a long while before Helen cried herself into a deep sleep, unaware of the shadow that lingered outsider her door, listening to her weep.

CHAPTER TWO

Gareth listened to Helen tug on the locked door handle. He was on the verge of going to his own chambers when she began to cry. He froze mid-step. It was such a quiet, sweet, sad noise. It reminded him of a time when he'd captured and caged a wild thrush.

The little bird had been stunned at first, quiet and unsure, before it began to sing a sad little song, a plea of mercy. The thrush had only lasted a few weeks in a cage before its chirps lost their wild charms. Gareth knew that he had to release the bird if he ever wished to hear its song again, but the fear of letting go struck him deep. He had worked hard to make the bird his own, and he didn't want to release his hard won prize. But he knew with certainty that the bird would lose its song. Finally, he'd had to set it free. The memory of letting it go was burned into his heart.

As the cage latch sprang open and the bird shot out of its prison, it fluttered away, and Gareth's heart fell. He would never hear it sing again.

But a minute later, he heard the distant trill slowly growing louder. The little thrush had returned. It perched on the edge of the garden wall, chattering away as though it had never been held prisoner. Perhaps Helen was like the thrush...needed to be kept caged for a time before he would release her, and maybe then she would return to him.

Gareth was twenty-seven and sole owner of a vast estate, but life had left him little to hope for. He'd lost his parents long ago, and his wife to childbirth when he was only twenty. He'd been a fool to marry so young, but he and Clarissa had been childhood sweethearts. After Clarissa and the babe had died, he sought ways to fill the bleak void in his heart that grew larger with each passing year. He gambled, drank—everything a man of leisure could afford— and still could not find peace. His restlessness had reared its ugly head when he had challenged Martin Banks to a duel.

Either he would lose the duel or be executed for killing Banks in an illegal duel. It should have ended tonight, but he'd been confounded by Helen. He'd been moved by her courage to take her brother's place. Like the songbird, she affected him deeply...in ways he had not begun to fully understand. He had to have her, had to hear her song in the whisper of his name, the sighs full of ecstasy, and the laugh of triumph from his own lips as he claimed her. She was a creature of sunlight, spirit, and innocence, and he craved her like he'd never craved anything in his life. He was a bastard to use her for his pleasure because her brother owed him. But damned if he didn't still desire her with a wild and unbridled hunger he hadn't felt since he'd last held his wife in his arms. He would have been lucky to recapture just one bit of that feeling again, but with Helen, it flooded through him, a tidal wave he could not stop, nor did he wish to.

When her crying stopped, and Gareth could hear no more sounds from her room, he headed toward his own bedchamber. Mary appeared at his side. She was a wizened woman in her early fifties and had been with Gareth's family since Gareth's mother was a bride.

"Might I have a word, Master Gareth?" she asked gravely, her voice low and disapproving. While Gareth had no interest in being lectured like a naughty schoolboy, he did not dare refuse her the right to chastise him for his wrongdoing. He had practically abducted the poor girl, after all.

"Yes Mary," he leaned heavily against the frame of the doorway to his own chambers.

"I know it has been awhile since you've had a woman in this house. Might I advise sending to Bath for gowns that suit her? It would not be proper for her to wear Mrs. Fairfax's clothes."

This remark astounded him. Did Mary think he'd brought home a bit of muslin? Not a woman worthy of compassion? He caught himself suddenly astonished that he'd wished to defend Helen's character. How had she wormed her way into his heart so quickly?

"I'm afraid I don't take your meaning," he growled at Mary, daring her to make another remark against Helen. After everything that had happened to her—most of it his fault—he felt protective of her.

Mary blinked, then narrowed her eyes with annoyance. "I meant no offense to the young lady by saying she was not good enough to wear Mrs. Fairfax's clothes, sir…rather I meant that she is a great deal taller than Lady Clarissa was, and her fairer hair and skin require a much different color in gowns, not to mention fashion has changed in the last seven years. If you would permit me, I will send for a better wardrobe for her tomorrow morning." Mary lifted her chin, crossing her arms with an annoyed expression, as if expecting him to growl again.

Gareth relaxed considerably. "Yes, do what you see fit. I care not for fashion, but if it would make her happy…" He trailed off, surprised that he was thinking of what would please Helen when at first she'd only been an object brought here to please him. It seemed he'd been quite moved by her tears.

"Do you wish for me to take a look at your injury?" Mary's eyes dropped to his bloodied arm.

He gave a short jerk of his head. "'Tis only a scratch. Miss Banks took it upon herself to shoot me."

"Shoot you?" His housekeeper's voice rose an octave. "And what, pray tell, were you doing to her that warranted such a reaction?"

He flashed her a weary, yet still charming grin. "Well, that's the thing. I challenged her brother to a duel, and she showed up dressed like him and took his place. She shot me, accidentally, I think, before I realized she wasn't a man."

"Well, if you think you're well enough…" She was still eyeing the wound with worry. "I think I'll send for the doctor tomorrow and have him look it over in any case. Goodnight, sir." Mary curtsied, the corners of her mouth twitching so slightly he wondered if he'd imagined it before she left him to his thoughts and he readied for bed.

He stripped off his bloodied shirt and poured some water into his basin. The wound was superficial. The bullet had barely grazed him. He chuckled softly as he recalled Helen's wide, horrified eyes as she ran to help him in the field. Her first time to fire a pistol and she had managed to graze him—not bad for a woman.

And what a woman she was. She was truly beautiful with her soft, yielding lips of a green girl, the swell of perfect breasts, and the curve of a slender waist out to her wider hips. Just made for his hands.

God…it has been too long since I've had a woman. Gareth almost moaned. Among the many vices he'd acquired since his wife's death, seduction of other women hadn't been one of them. He hadn't the will or desire to bed any woman he'd come across in the last seven years. Yet, the mere thought of Helen beneath him in his bed, golden waves of hair rippling out around her in rays of condensed sunlight, made him shake with desire. What pleasure he would have when he took her that first time. Her sheath would squeeze him tight as a fist, and he knew the pleasure would be beyond compare. It had taken every bit of restraint he possessed to do no more than bring her to climax with his hand. His cock tightened in his breeches, shoving hard against the buttons.

He would have to control himself. She was a virgin. He had no doubt of that, not after he'd kissed her in the drawing room. She had been dewy-eyed with the innocent desire of an untouched maiden, yet she'd responded with a sensual hunger that marked her for a future as a great lover to a lucky man. She would learn just how good it felt to have him deep inside her while his lips drank from the sweetness of her mouth. Perhaps, he might at last find the pleasure he sought, after having had it torn from him seven years ago.

Gareth finished cleaning his shoulder and dressed the wound with a light bandage. As he settled into his own bed, he expected to dream of Helen and how he would seduce her come morning.

Instead, his dreams were haunted by the caged thrush and its fight for freedom, trilling a sad song into the murky depths of his unconsciousness.

Helen woke well rested and refreshed, so much so that she almost forgot the troubles from earlier that morning. But the moment her eyes took in the foreign bed lit by sunlight, she remembered where she was. Helen slid out from under the covers to stand, the wood floor cool beneath her bare feet. She washed her face in the water basin and went to the armoire to see what clothes she might find. As much as she had enjoyed the freedom of her brother's attire, it was not wise to put it on again.

She needed a clear mind to deal with Gareth. She faced this truth with the light of day heavy upon her. The bargain they'd struck early in the morning had to be undone. Surely he would realize that after his temper had cooled and he'd rested. There was no need to keep her here, not when he could have his pick of the ladies of Bath.

Pressing her fingers to her lips, she could swear she still felt his kiss. Her memories of the early morning were merely exaggerated dreams. What they'd done together, the way they'd embraced, touched...it hadn't been that deliciously wonderful had it? Yes, that was a dream, no doubt spurred on by her anxiety of the situation.

The only thing left for her to do was decide how to tell Gareth she meant to break the bargain they'd struck and convince him to let her return home. Excuses would have to be made in order to hide where she'd been. Perhaps she could say she was ill and stayed at a friend's house... But what friend did she have who would reinforce the lie? It was unlikely that would happen, and that wasn't her only problem. She would have to find a reputable means of repaying Martin's debts. In order to do that, she must return to Bath immediately, and she would not do it garbed in men's clothing. Her family's name was already shamed enough by Martin's gambling debts, she could not add to it.

The armoire was full of dresses, each lovely yet simple. The cuts and styles were a few years out of date, but the stitching and fabrics were far finer than she was used to. She chose a pale cerulean gown that had van-dyked sleeves and a modest neckline. It was too short in the skirts, but Helen didn't mind. She dressed in a light white chemise, petticoats, and stays and was in the act of donning the gown when her door was unlocked and Mary entered.

"Good morning, Miss Banks. I trust you slept well?" Mary came over to help her dress.

"I did, thank you," she replied shyly. She'd had to let her ladies' maid, Olivia, go a few months ago. Servants were far too costly to maintain without money when she and her brother could barely afford to eat. Mary made quick work of letting out the hem of the dress with a small pair of sewing scissors.

"The master has permitted me to send for gowns more suitable to your height and coloring. They'll be here later today," Mary said as she gestured for Helen to sit in front of the vanity table.

"I do not wish to inconvenience him," Helen said, distressed to hear that this might in some way further the great debt between them. Mary shushed her as she brushed Helen's hair and began to style it.

Mary seemed able to read her thoughts. "It was at my request. He thinks little of the expense, and it is no inconvenience."

Can I allow him to do this for me? The thought of lovely gowns, a whole pile of them just for her...it was almost too much. And she hated herself for wanting them, even just to look at.

"There now, a vision of loveliness. Do not let the master muss it up," she warned with a secretive smile. Helen blushed, her skin radiating with the implications of Mary's warning.

When Helen turned and stared at herself in the mirror, she marveled at the style the housekeeper had chosen. Mary had pulled her locks back loosely into a rippling coil much in the Grecian style. Several loose curls fell against the back of her neck, and a matching cerulean ribbon threaded about her hair held it all in place.

"I did not think anyone save the master woke at such an early hour. The breakfast will not be ready for another hour. Perhaps you would care to see the gardens?" Mary suggested as she ushered Helen out of the bedchamber.

"I'm sure the gardens will be lovely," she said, but when her stomach rumbled, she blushed in shame.

"Oh dear, come to the kitchens with me and I'll see you get something into that belly of yours before you go out." The housekeeper tugged one of her curls playfully, the gesture so warm and fond that Helen blinked back tears. Her mother used to do that—tug a curl and kiss her cheek.

Helen started to protest, but the hunger pains only grew and she didn't see a point in fighting. Mary ushered her out of the bedchamber and led her towards the kitchens.

Gareth's house, so haunting and dark at night, was a different creature altogether in the light of day. Sun broke through the many windows, lighting up paintings of pastoral scenes and gardens which decorated the walls. It was as though the house's inhabitants had wanted to feel they were forever in the gardens, even while inside the walls. And yet, despite its beauty, something felt hollow here. Helen thought of when she'd been a child and she'd found an abandoned nest in the late fall. This house had that same feel…as though it, too, had lost those who'd once dwelt within its walls.

"Mary, has this house always been so lonely?" She knew it was impertinent to ask, but her curiosity demanded an answer.

"The master lost his wife and child seven years ago. He was only a lad then, barely twenty. The house has been quiet since my lady's passing." Mary sighed heavily as though it pained her to speak of the loss.

"Mr. Fairfax is only twenty-seven?" She was astounded by this. He did not look old, but his voice, his gaze, his physical presence seemed to her to be so worldly, so experienced. To think, he was only six years her senior. Helen repressed the sudden flare of irritation at his treating her as though she were a mere babe at times. Then her irritation faded in the wake of a tremor at how he'd kissed her in her chamber. Maybe he didn't think of her as being so young after all.

The kitchens were bustling with busy servants, and Helen lingered in the doorway, afraid to intrude. Mary gathered a couple of cookies and ushered her back into the hallway. Helen took the treats and nibbled on them as she followed the housekeeper to a door at the rear of the house.

"Ah, here we are. The gardens are just beyond. Should you fancy a longer walk, there is a nice meadow outside. But do not stray far. It is easy to get lost. We are quite far from any village." Mary shoved her gently out the door.

The second Mary was gone, Helen started walking, keeping her pace slow as she finished the last of the cookies and put a hand to her stomach, relishing the satisfied feeling. She had the strangest urge to run, to escape. Knowing Gareth was somewhere close made her feel…vulnerable, exposed. Early that morning, she'd been certain she could handle him and be happy to share his bed. But sleeping had returned her good sense. She wasn't prepared for a joining with a man, especially not one like Gareth. He'd barge into her heart, steal it away, and leave her body restless for him and his kisses for the rest of her life. A woman simply could not afford that sort of problem, not when she'd likely have to beg on the streets to save what remained of her family.

She paused to cup flowers in her hands and breathe their scent in. But she never forgot for a moment that she should be working up the courage to speak to Gareth and break off their agreement.

He must be up and about somewhere on the estate, if Mary's words were any evidence. Helen still felt unprepared to see him again. It would be too easy to get lost in the memory of his mouth on hers, his hand stroking between her thighs in that dark, hot place. As though she'd summoned her own demon of passion, the spot between her legs throbbed steadily—insistently—for Gareth's expert touch.

She finally located the garden's exit, deciding it might be better to get further away from the house for a while and hoping the fresh air would clear her head.

The exit was a stone archway with a wooden door covered in climbing ivy. Helen dug around the slick ivy leaves to find the handle and cracked the door open. Beyond it, she found a sprawling scene of beautiful land, trees dotting the edges of the rolling meadows, and azure skies stretching to the heavens themselves. As she passed through the archway, she had the strangest sense that she was free of Gareth and the binding of their devil's bargain. Behind her was the house and his control, ahead of her was only open land. She could go where she wished…

I'm a fool to think he won't come after me. He would find her, she had no doubt, but the illusion of freedom was something she wouldn't take for granted, even for so short a time.

Fluffy white shapes dotted a distant sloping hill. *They must be sheep.* Her heart skipped a beat at the beauty. It reminded her so much of her childhood home, a small cottage, far away from here, which had abutted an estate as grand as this. Surely she had taken a wrong turn outside the garden gate. This had to be paradise, not Gareth's lands.

Damn Martin and his gambling. If only he'd controlled himself. I'd never have ended up here, seen this place, or kissed Gareth.

Helen was halfway through the meadow when it occurred to her that she ought to seek shelter in the trees where he could not see her, if she wished to have her moment alone to clear her head. Given that

Gareth had locked her in her room last night, he might think she intended to escape if he saw her in the meadow.

She changed direction, walking parallel to the house as she headed toward the nearest copse of trees. She turned back once more, pausing to see the house one last time before she left. The soft snap of twigs and the brush of cloth made her spin back around. Gareth was lounging against a tree six feet away from her.

"Taking a walk, Helen?" The way he caressed her name made her shiver. He was dressed in tan breeches and a waistcoat of dark navy blue, so at odds with the greens and umber browns of the woods behind him.

"Good Morning, Mr. Fairfax." She gave a nod of greeting but looked away from his openly admiring gaze. It was all too familiar to the way he'd looked upon her last night when he'd pinned her against the bedpost and... Heat infused her cheeks and flashed beneath the surface of her skin.

He shifted away from the tree he'd been leaning against. "Please, call me Gareth. You are looking well. Blushing suits you."

"Er... Thank you." She wasn't sure if she ought to have thanked him for such a comment, but she did it anyway, trying to maintain a pretense of calm. Her eyes scanned the area on either side of him, trying to determine the best route to get around him. He was blocking her best path.

"I should like to continue my walk...Gareth. Would you let me pass?" She finally summoned the courage to look him in the eye.

It was a mistake.

His eyes burned her, invisible flames flicking over her skin, heating her from the inside out. The throbbing started between her thighs again and she clenched them together, but the pressure only made the throbbing worse.

"And let you run off and get lost? My darling Helen, I'd much rather you stay here so I don't have to find you later." The grin of devilish delight playing with his lips was far too charming and far too dangerous. He took a step closer.

Helen's heartbeat increased. If she ran now, would he dare to grab her? It would be so uncivilized. Yet there was something distinctly *uncivilized* about him. The predatory way he stalked her and the primal way he'd taken control of her body earlier that morning in her chamber set her ablaze inside. Helen darted to the left, choosing the opening between Gareth and the tree. He lunged, catching her easily by wrapping one arm around her waist. She was too startled to scream as he backed her up against the rough bark. Her hands clenched at his chest, catching the smooth fabric of his waistcoat. He gripped her waist, holding her firm and preventing her from escaping him.

"Helen …" he whispered, his voice strangely soothing, calming. "I'm not going to hurt you. I made a promise, and I keep my promises." A ghost of a smile hovered at his mouth. "But I am going to kiss you."

Her traitorous body relaxed in his hold. Her eyes drifted shut, her head tilting upward for his kiss. But his lips never touched hers. Instead they trailed softly from her neck down to the swell of her breasts. Her breathing deepened, her chest rising to meet his exploring mouth. With each inhalation, she struggled to stay above the drowning sense of dizziness that his touch roused in her. He cupped one of the tender mounds, his thumb circling her hardened nipple through the fabric of her gown. He pinched the bud and Helen forgot breathing all together. His eyes were lowered, studying her reaction—the way her skin flushed as he continued to tease and torture the sensitive peak. Helen was fascinated by his intense expression, the way his lips were slightly parted, his breath rougher, his eyes half-lidded but their gleam sharp. When his fingers pinched her nipple again, she gasped, drawing his focus back up to her face.

"You are so responsive, so alive," he murmured, his thumb caressing her cheek. "You don't even know what that does to me, do you?"

Helen swallowed, her mouth dry and incapable of forming words.

Gareth's hands wound around her waist, pulling her away from the tree and toward the edge of the meadow.

"Sit," he urged gently.

Still entranced by the way he kept her spellbound with his soft, arousing words and touches, she allowed him to help her down onto the ground. He pressed her shoulders, urging her to lie back. The grass bent beneath her when he cradled one arm behind her head as a firm pillow.

"What are we doing?" she whispered, studying

his face, the sunlight haloing him as he leaned over her.

"Getting acquainted," he replied, as though what they were doing was the most normal thing in all the world.

"Wouldn't that entail you courting me by bringing me flowers and sitting in the parlor under the watchful eyes of a chaperone?" She was half joking, trying to fight off the tingle of nervousness that made its way through her body with small tremors.

His rich laugh made her smile. He could be teasing and playful then. Knowing that eased more of the tension inside her and she relaxed.

"Do you want flowers? I can promise you a field of wildflowers, a garden, even a hothouse. Whatever you desire, it is yours. But no chaperones and no parlors. I want you, want to know your body and the way it responds to mine." His earnestness surprised her. He seemed as baffled by his answering hunger for her.

She squirmed, trying to stop his hand from pushing up her skirts, but he gently pushed her hand away. Helen's eyes widened as his other hand slid beneath her gown and up her left thigh. The dress's fabric rose obligingly at his hand's command, taking her petticoats with it. Helen's mouth parted as she gasped in shock and her sudden fear of vulnerability. She was terrified of his hand on her bare thigh and even more scared by how she wanted him to keep moving his palm higher even though she guessed where it would lead. Did all women feel this way when first touched by a man, torn between desperation to escape and the need for more?

Gareth's face blocked out the bright sky. Would he give her pleasure like last night?

"Do not fear me, Helen." It almost sounded like a plea.

But if Helen knew anything about a man like Gareth Fairfax, she knew he was not the sort of man to beg. Rather, the hunger that flamed behind his dark brown eyes explained everything. He needed her body, needed to have her accept whatever it was he wished to do. What could a woman say to that? *Yes, take me, take all of me?* She wasn't nearly ready for that sort of surrender to him. The thought was erased as Gareth's head descended toward hers.

His lips found hers. She was lost to the pleasure of his tongue dancing with hers but still aware of his hand as it parted her legs and slid through the slit in her drawers. That first brush of his fingertips on her hot flesh burned them both, her with a hiss and him with a groan. Helen shifted restlessly as wetness pooled between her thighs. He moved deeper, finding the swollen flesh tender and yearning. He stroked her once, twice, opening her further to him. She shivered in pleasure as he continued. Her legs twisted and shifted as she adjusted to the strange sensation of his invading touch. It was as though he was caressing the innermost part of her. Each slow thrust of his fingers was a delicious teasing. Gareth's mouth left hers again to lay kisses along the lines of her collarbone and down to the heavy swell of her breasts.

A pain grew deep within her, a hunger between

her legs, the same desire that she'd felt this morning in her room. She clutched Gareth's shoulders. As though he understood her body's needs, his fingers sunk deeper into her, and she let out a small cry of pleasure mingled with fear. Pinpricks of tiny explosions burst forth, sending tremors outward along her limbs. She clung to him, her violent quaking subsiding against the strength of his embrace.

He withdrew his hand, pulling her petticoats and gown back down over her hips and legs. He kissed her again, the meeting of mouths softer than before, as though he sought to maintain the intimacy of that moment—their closeness and the isolation they found together in the meadow. He held her against him and Helen breathed in his scent. Sandalwood, leather, and something uniquely belonging to him, intoxicating as an opiate. The breeze moved the grass around them like waves of an emerald sea. For a brief moment, Helen thought they were the only two people in this paradise, and that no world existed outside.

"Do I still frighten you?" Gareth asked, his tone teasing as he stroked her cheek.

Helen, spellbound by the sensations he'd created in her moments ago, was speechless for a second. She leaned into his caress, unable to deny herself the pleasure of his touch. She could not escape him, and she was beginning to want to stay. But a part of her still feared him, the way he made her want things she knew she could never have, like happiness with a man like him. She remembered the fire in his eyes as he demanded the debt be paid. He would claim it— claim her—and that did frighten her. What would happen when he was done and she'd been foolish enough to let herself fall for him?

"I believe you will always frighten me," she admitted. But it was a different sort of fear, not one of harm to the body, but devastation to the heart.

His laugh was low and rough. "You present me with a challenge then. I shall spend our time together wooing you into trusting me." He fingered one of her loosened curls, wearing a boyish smile. "I rather like you, Helen."

She bit her lip, the words *I rather like you, too* hung on the tip of her tongue, unspoken.

He got to his feet, brushing grass off his breeches. "Should we return to the house and see if Mary has breakfast ready?"

She wobbled for a few seconds as he pulled her to her feet. Her legs trembled, still reverberating with the memory of what he'd done to her and how her body had reacted. Echoes of pleasure still worked their way through her in little flushes and the twitching of her inner muscles. He held out an arm, which she leaned on, grateful for the support.

The house was abuzz with the flutter of servants when they returned. Maids were dusting shelves and polishing candlesticks. Footmen were stretching their legs by running errands at Mary's bidding. She stood in the main hall, issuing orders better than a British General. Gareth nodded in greeting as they passed her on their way to the dining room. She smiled, brief but warm, before dashing off to chastise a clumsy footman who'd tripped on the edge of a carpet and spilled the basin of water he'd been carrying.

The table was decorated with plates of fruit, eggs, kippers, and various jams for spreading on a stack of warm toast. Helen's stomach growled at the sight of food. Even though she'd stuffed herself on cookies an hour ago, the sight of these new dishes renewed her hunger. Over the last few months, she had survived on small portions of bread and water, just to be able to get by. She'd taken to giving her brother the larger share of whatever meals they could afford. Gareth pulled out a chair for her next to his own seat at the head of the table. Helen reached for the nearest piece of toast but froze, remembering her manners. Gareth had not yet made a move towards the food. His eyes were scanning a stack of letters brought in by a servant. He glanced up, noticing her stillness.

"Do not wait for me. Please eat." He smiled warmly at her. She had to stop herself before she smiled back. He was a different person from early this morning. Then, he'd been a haunted, troubled man, burdened by anger and frustration. Now he seemed... kind. Even in the meadow, his touch had been soft, insistent, too, but not brutal...not like what she'd expected.

Helen filled a plate with a balance of fruits, eggs, and toast, enjoying the variety. There was a flare of excitement in her at being able to eat as much as she wanted. Their fortune had been so slight that meals had been meager of late, and she'd been forced to convince Martin that she wasn't nearly as hungry as he was so that he might have a fuller belly. For the first time since her father died, she was able to worry only about herself, about what she needed. Her stomach grumbled again, and Helen eyed the stack of toast thoughtfully before quickly snatching another piece and adding it to her plate.

This strange sense of comfort and ease made her less and less willing to fight against Gareth and his desires. If she liked what happened in the meadow, she would probably like other things he might do to her. Well, if she was being truly honest, she hadn't just liked it. She'd reveled in it. It might be worth it —his physical pleasure traded for food and clothing. A cold thought struck her. Was she no better than the type of women she'd feared she would become? Surely not. Gareth didn't treat her like she was that sort of woman, but still... Helen shook her head slightly to rid herself of that unpleasant thought and turned her attention back to the food.

Gareth read his letters as he ate, seemingly oblivious to her study of him. She thought perhaps her mind had exaggerated the marble carved features of perfection on his face, but they were just as she had remembered. The sunlight played with his hair, revealing a hint of chocolate brown amidst the rich russet. His hands were large and strong, the fingers deftly breaking the seals of his letters. Those were the same hands that had brought unspeakable pleasure to her only a short while ago. A delicious little shiver ran through her at the memory.

When Gareth finished his breakfast, he bid her a good day with a genteel bow, lifting her hand to press his lips on the inside of her wrist. Her pulse jumped at the intimate contact.

She was fascinated by him, like a helpless

minnow spying its first shiny lure in the stream. Helen wanted to follow him, to see where he would go and what he would do. Would he want to kiss her or pleasure her again? Gareth was halfway out the door when he paused and Helen bumped into his back. He looked over his shoulder at her as though surprised to find her so close.

"You mean to follow me, Helen? I do not expect you to. You are free to go about the house and gardens as you wish."

Helen frowned. Was he dismissing her? Did he mean to leave her alone while he went about his day? The thought saddened her. Perhaps she was not a good companion and he would soon tire of her. As a twin, she craved companionship, and didn't like too much time alone. She didn't need to be speaking to someone every minute of the day, but she liked another person in her presence. Perhaps Gareth was the opposite and did not wish to have her around.

Her unhappy silence affected him enough that he reached out for her arm and tilted his head to indicate she should accompany him.

"Come along then. I'm off to the stables. It is a fine day for riding."

"You have horses?" She was all smiles again, memories of her youth flooding through her. They'd once owned a pair of stout draft horses, and she and Martin used to ride them in the summer.

"Of course I have horses, my darling. How do you think my coach brought you here?"

He was teasing her, she could see it in his eyes. She liked it when he was playful. He must feel something for her, however small, if he joked with her. One of Martin's boyhood friends used to tug her hair, and her mother said that men often treated the women they liked in such a fashion.

"Do you know how to ride?"

"I do, but not sidesaddle, I'm afraid," she admitted. Her father hadn't bothered with teaching her the niceties expected of gentle bred ladies, at least when it came to riding. Since her mother died when she was a child, she'd been without the feminine guidance that would have taught her such things.

"That is well, for I got rid of the only sidesaddle I had years ago."

"Because your wife passed away?" She regretted the words the moment they came out. "I'm sorry. I did not mean to..." she was flustered, her face warm with embarrassment.

"Do not worry. I have mourned Clarissa, my wife, and am at peace with her death. You may speak about her if you wish. It will not cause me pain, I assure you." Despite the polite smile that curved his lips, there was a guarded wariness in his face that said there was still a twist in his heart at the mention of his late wife.

"You loved her very much." Helen saw it in his eyes, the way the sadness there formed dark shadows. Losing someone you loved often left a stain upon the soul.

"She was my friend. Not many men are fortunate enough to have wives who lay claim to their hearts and their minds, not just as lovers but also as friends. It's a loss not easy to recover from. I mourn the way we used to talk late into the night and ride together on lazy afternoons." He gave a little shake of his head, as though to dispel the creeping melancholy. "We were happy when many around us were not so fortunate. I'll likely never know that sense of joy again."

Helen bit her bottom lip, pain clamping its vice-like claws on her own heart, threatening to rip it asunder. Gareth was a wounded man still, no matter that he believed he'd moved on. Everything about him was becoming clearer, he was desperate to feel, to live again, and using her, even as a temporary companion, must be one way in which he was trying to find solace. She did not feel pity, but rather it filled her with compassion.

With false cheeriness, he gestured to the stairs. "Would you like to go and change into a riding habit?"

"Yes. I shall only be a moment," she promised.

Once Helen was properly attired for riding, they left the house and approached the building next to it. It was a small but well-kept stable with four stalls for the four horses he owned. They were all matching bays with tall heads and long, lean legs, nothing like the draft horses she'd ridden as a child.

Even though she didn't want to cause him distress, she still wanted to get to know him. If she were to stay here with him, she'd have to understand him better. "If you no longer miss your wife, why haven't you remarried?"

How could this man, so blessed in looks and fortune, not find another wife, one who would delight in pleasing him? Gareth smiled, though it was little and pained. His eyes moved from the horse to her. She read the truth there. Clarissa couldn't be replaced and he hadn't wanted to try.

"I got used to Clarissa's absence after a few years, but I've become restless. Nothing eases me anymore, nothing gives me peace." He spoke softly, more to himself as though the revelation was one he'd never dared to voice aloud. His confession was like opening a book, the pages revealing a glimpse of his secrets. She craved to read more of his soul, to come to know him the way he knew only himself.

Helen wished to comfort him, so she put a hand on his arm. "Try to love again. Love settle's a person's heart."

He shook his head. "No. Love destroys. It rips you clean in two and devastates you. I would never go looking for that again."

Gareth looked at her, her blue eyes gazing at him in pity. Did she not know what she was asking of him? Love was hard to find, hard to earn, and hard to keep. He reached up to tug one of her curls playfully, wanting to rid his mind of the thoughts she'd put there. His actions made her wrinkle her nose in disapproval. The urge to hold her was too strong to resist. He tugged her into his arms, relishing the feel of her body flush against his.

She was growing ever more receptive to his kisses. He let her mouth guide his, let her explore his chest, his arms, his back before she locked her hands around his neck. Her fingertips brushed the back of his neck and stroked his hair. He loved how quickly she opened up to him, how she let him instruct her in the ways of seduction.

The feeling of her touch on his skin made him shiver. She was a quick learner. Gareth wanted to part her legs again, like he'd done in the meadow, but the stables were no place for such an activity. Instead he teased her breasts through the fabric of her gown until he felt her grow breathless. He hardened, his groin aching with need, but he could not take her, not until she asked for him. He could have kissed and touched her for hours.

"My apologies, sir!" A groom, who'd walked into the stables, apologized profusely as he scrambled away, overturning a bucket of feed in his haste to depart.

Helen stifled an embarrassed giggle and buried her face in his chest as though to hide herself from the world. Gareth found himself laughing, too. It was a loud, rich laugh, one he hadn't made in years. What was she doing to him? In a mere matter of a day, she had turned his world upside down. She was open and honest about herself and her life. And brave. He couldn't forget that, either, the way she'd risked her life to save her brother's knowing she would die. What woman of his acquaintance would have dared to risk her life? None that he knew. Helen was different. She was real and beautiful and so full of life. Each time he looked at her, something inside him seemed to shake off a century's worth of dust and awaken. Being around her made him feel alive.

"Let's get the horses ready. We should get a ride in while the day is young." Gareth reluctantly pried her away from his chest and set about saddling the horses.

They rode at a nice canter for nearly an hour, over the meadow, down the hill, and through the neighboring lands. Gareth chuckled as Helen rode her mare through a flock of panicked sheep. They both nearly fell out of their saddles with laughter as they watched the wooly creatures bolt in all directions to avoid being trampled by her horse. The sheep gathered rebelliously into a flock several yards away, bleating melodramatically at having been attacked.

"Heavens! That was quite a ride," Helen said as she watched the sheep shifting restlessly as her horse stomped and huffed.

"I daresay, the farmer, Mr. Pennysworth, won't be pleased to find we've been scaring his beasts. Come, let's away, Helen," He chuckled and lightly tugged the reins of his horse, guiding it to turn around.

Gareth watched Helen the entire time they were out riding. He could not keep his eyes off the halo of her golden hair or the mischievous grin as she drove towards the sheep. Her little laugh was music to him, music he'd been missing for years.

Sing my little thrush, please sing to me. She was beautiful, she was perfect, and he would have to let her go. That brother of hers would eventually show up, and Gareth would have to deal with him when the time came. Damned if he knew what to do with Martin Banks. The fool might still insist on the duel, now over Helen's honor. What a mess he was in. His eyes strayed to Helen, and her easy smile made all of the problems with his choice to have her fade. She was worth the trouble. He knew he could not keep her for long. Ambrose's words came back to him. He was ruining her for her brother's debts. Debts she shouldn't have to pay, and he'd destroyed all chances of her making a good match. On the field after the duel that hadn't mattered to him, in fact he'd relished the thought of hurting Banks by saddling him with a sister who would never make a match. But now…now he saw he was only hurting Helen, a brave, innocent woman who didn't deserve any of this. Yet there was no way to undo the damage he'd done.

Marriage was out of the question. He had nothing to offer her besides his name and his body, and he knew only too well that a woman like Helen would need his heart to survive a marriage. For him, it was seduction, plain and simple. He had no right to anything else. He'd lost his right to love a long time ago. God would not give him a second chance, not after blessing him with Clarissa. That sort of love, he was sure, came only once. He had his turn and lost. Helen was nothing more than a cruel reminder of what he could never have.

CHAPTER THREE

Helen spent the remainder of the day exploring the house, reading in the expansive library, and being spoiled by the numerous cooks in the kitchen, who were more than delighted to let her taste pies, pastries, and other dishes they were preparing. Gareth had to leave on a business related matter but had assured her he would return in time for dinner. Helen found the house felt empty with his departure at first, but Mary soon distracted her with activities. She was allowed to play freely on the pianoforte in the music room, she was encouraged to explore the gardens, and she was positively forced to try on gown after gown once they arrived late in the afternoon from Bath. About halfway through the day, Helen was sure this was an elaborate and wonderful dream, and that eventually, she would wake to find herself back in Bath, ever watchful of her brother and their meager finances.

Once Mary had finished fitting all of the new gowns, she left Helen to her own devices. The day was still clear and fine and the warm sun was setting in the western sky as Helen entered the gardens once more. She found a stout tree near the garden wall and decided to climb it to better see the sunset. Climbing was something more suited for a young child, not a woman of one and twenty, but she couldn't find it in herself to care. Here, she was free to do as she wished, to eat, to play, to laugh, even to climb. In this private world, she had been swept away by the sense of timelessness. She could do whatever she wanted, and at the moment, she planned to climb a tree to get a better glimpse of the reddening skies beyond the gardens.

Returning to her chamber, she quickly donned her brother's breeches and shirt. It was the best attire for climbing. Her new white muslin gown would have been completely ruined. Helen shared her brother's athletic build and found it easy to grasp the lowest branches and hoist herself up. The bark was rough beneath her palms, but she ignored the sting of the minor scrapes on her sensitive skin. By the time she stopped ascending, she had a fair view of the sunset over the garden wall.

The sun was now a crimson apple hanging low on the horizon as though waiting to be plucked. Thick beams of gold light tickled the waving grasses of the meadow, deepening the emerald colors. It was that one hour of the day so often missed during the bustle of activity, when the world seemed frozen in that golden span of time. A hush descended over the land, bird chatter was quieter, and no breezes whipped the branches or grass. There was only a soft silence, like when a mother puts her babe to sleep in the late afternoon. The air was filled with the promise of what night might bring, yet the flurry of activity for the evening had not begun. It was a sacred time.

"How the devil did you get up there?" Gareth's voice boomed.

Helen jerked, nearly falling from the branch she balanced on. She glanced down, seeing him at the base of the tree, looking up at her. Ten feet separated her from Gareth and the ground. It was no great distance, really.

"I climbed, of course." She laughed at his look of surprise, her heart sliding down from her throat and back into her chest as she steadied herself again. "How did you find me?"

His brows drew down into a slight frown. One of the gardeners saw you come out here in your brother's clothes. He was worried you were planning to leave, so he kept track of where you went.

This time, it was she who frowned. "You've had your servants watching me?"

"Well…" He glanced away, guilty. "Not really. I merely told them you were not to leave the grounds without me. It was more the fact that you were walking around in breeches that got the man's attention, rather than my order for him to keep an eye on you," Gareth answered.

"Oh," she exhaled. It did make sense. She'd jumped to conclusions about him and had been wrong—well, not entirely—but still wrong enough to feel the uncomfortable weight of her own guilt at making such suppositions.

"Shall I call the head gardener for his ladder?"

She sighed. "No, I can get down. I just wanted to see the sunset." Her eyes once more returned to the peach colored skies aflame around the setting sun. She could have stayed there forever, watching the slowly changing colors, forgetting every worry that hung heavy on her soul.

The tree gave a little shake and branches whispered around her. She glanced back down to see Gareth climbing up toward her. He balanced himself at the fork of the large branch she was sitting on and the base of the tree. He tested the branch to see if it would hold his weight. There was a single moment, when he raised his eyes to her face, that she saw something in his expression that gave her a little shiver. Desire and contentment tinged with desperation as he gazed upon her, as though she were a great prize held high above his reach. No one had *ever* looked at her that way. She knew enough women who would have used that look to their advantage, but her first instinct was to go to him, to kiss away the sorrow in his eyes and the tightness of his mouth. Even though he'd ruined her, she couldn't resist him.

When he was satisfied the tree would hold him, he opened his arms to her. Without thinking, Helen slid over to nestle herself back against him as they watched the sunset together.

"How was your day?" His warm breath stirred the curls of hair dangling against her neck.

"Wonderful. Absolutely wonderful. It has been so long since…" She caught herself.

"So long since what?" His lips pressed lightly against her cheek. She shut her eyes, wishing she could tell him, but shame kept her quiet.

"Tell me, Helen." Her name on his lips weakened her resolve to remain silent.

Silence fell between them as she hesitated. He didn't press her to speak. He simply held onto her, as though they had countless hours to simply exist together in the same sphere, a single word unneeded. It was this sense of comfort he created that made her able to trust him with the vulnerable truth of her situation.

"It has been so long since I had a day where I could do as I wished, not have to save my food so Martin could have more, not have to mend yet another tear in my only shawl, not have to fear the whispers and societal slights against me and my brother at the assembly rooms. A day where I could be myself." She felt the telltale burn of a blush, but she couldn't stop it.

Gareth, whose hand had been rubbing up and down her back, stilled the movement. For a breathless moment, she feared he'd move away.

"How long has your brother been losing money at the tables?"

"For nearly three months. He only waited a month after our father died before he started frequenting the gambling hells. We started out with so little. He claimed he could win enough to keep us well situated in Bath. We had only just moved here a few weeks after Papa died. We took a pair of small rooms with a low rent, but Martin said we needed more. That's when he began haunting the card tables."

Gareth's hands rubbed her hips, the touch soothing, rather than erotic. "I take it he never listened to you when you asked him to stop."

"No. The first few times he returned with his pockets empty, I fought with him. Our rows were terrible, and we said unforgivable things to each other. After that, he started slipping out after I retired to bed each night. I knew what he was up to, of course. In the mornings, his eyes were red and his clothes rumpled as though he'd slept in them. It was so obvious, but there was little I could do to stop him." Helen's voice broke as raw, painful emotions ripped through her.

Gareth said nothing and his silence worried her. Would he cast her out? Now that he knew the truth? He caught her chin, turning her face towards his. His eyes were warm and compassionate as he breathed two words.

"My darling…" He kissed her softly, sweetly. "I'm so sorry."

It was just the sort of kiss she had thought would be her first, one full of emotion where heat was secondary. Yet there was passion behind the tenderness. She could feel it in the depth of his lips and the warmth of his arm that encircled his waist.

Gareth finally broke the kiss, but he rested his forehead against hers, keeping her close as though he didn't desire to separate himself from her. "We should get down. Mary will be angry if we are late for dinner."

He climbed down first and held out his arms for her to jump. The invitation to give herself to him was beyond compelling. She resisted, climbing down the last few branches on her own until she saw the hurt in his eyes. Hesitating, she studied his face. His expression was so different than before. Pleading glimmered in his eyes, and she let herself surrender to him, allowing him to help her down the last branch to the ground.

Mary kidnapped Helen the moment they were both inside.

"Look at the state of the pair of you! Covered in leaves and heaven knows what else," she chastised, but Helen thought she saw a glimmer of a smile on Mary's lips.

"We've been climbing trees." Gareth flashed Helen a conspiratorial grin.

"I can *see* that, sir." Mary retorted. She plucked Helen's arm off his and took her to her bedchamber, muttering under her breath about trees "being a gardener's concern". Helen bit her tongue to stop from laughing.

"Now, let's get you cleaned up and into a proper evening gown."

Mary helped her wash up and change. Helen wore a fine burgundy evening gown with short sleeves. It had a very low neckline, which Helen kept tugging up until Mary caught her.

"Let the gown be, my dear. You have a fine figure, show it to your advantage."

"But it's dreadfully low," Helen whispered in a scandalized tone.

Mary raised a wicked eyebrow.

"Yes it is."

Helen's cheeks heated but she realized it wouldn't matter. At this rate, she'd likely not be wearing the gown past dessert. She hadn't forgotten the incident in the meadow earlier that day and the promise that had lingered in Gareth's eyes. Tonight he would seduce her, fully and completely. It was inevitable and she saw little point in fighting it, especially when she knew she wanted it just as badly as he did. She was quickly becoming addicted to the ecstasy of his touch.

Mary handed Helen a gold shawl that matched her fair hair and propelled the girl into the hall. Mary watched her go on to the dining room alone. She knew Helen was an innocent young lady, and soon her master would pluck the ripe fruit that the child was unknowingly offering, but she did not pass judgment. She had known her master since he was a babe in the cradle, and he had a kind heart and a gentle soul.

These past few years, he'd fallen from a good path. But from the moment that Helen passed through the doorway, he'd been changing. Mary was not a gambling woman, but she would wager that before all this was over, her master would do right by the girl. It was clear he was exceedingly fond of her, and she was already twining him about her finger without even realizing it. Gareth Fairfax just might be falling in love again. Perhaps there would be another wedding and another baby to fill the house. Mary let out a wistful sigh, smoothed her skirts, and headed in the direction of the kitchens.

The dining room glowed beneath the evening sun, which gilded everything in its path. The effect was like something from a fairy tale dream. Helen couldn't believe how beautiful the light was as it illuminated the table and the feast which had been laid out before her. The abundance of food was startling. She hadn't seen so much since...well, ever. After months of watching her finances, to see such luxury, the food too much for two people, her smile faltered.

"Surely we don't need this much..." she briefly closed her eyes before opening them. "I didn't speak to you this afternoon about my situation in order to provoke such lavish treatment."

He eyed her seriously. "Nothing here is wasted, I assure you. Now, come and sit by me."

Gareth gave her a small smile when she crossed

the room. The warmth of his hands seeped into her bare skin when they brushed her shoulders as he seated her. Despite her worry about his subdued manner, she managed to eat the delicious dish of duck she'd been served. She sipped her wine, knowing that too much of it gave her dreadful headaches in the morning, but she felt the fortification of a little bit of spirits might help her relax tonight.

To her delight, the dessert served was raspberries. She speared one with her fork, but as she raised it up, she noticed Gareth watching her with heavy lidded eyes. He was lounging back in his chair, one hand lazily holding his glass of wine, the other stroking circles on the crimson tablecloth. Like a lazy lion, he seemed content to watch his prey flounder and panic, wondering how he would strike. She slowly slipped the raspberry into her mouth, swallowing hard as she forgot to chew.

"There are better ways to eat those." His voice was smooth as velvet and dark as night. It cast a spell on her, slowly drowning her in the thick sensuality of the look that accompanied his words. The world around them seemed to darken and then fade, leaving them alone in the decadent dining room. She was all too aware his intentions had nothing to do with the proper consumption of raspberries. It was a game, and she wanted to play.

Helen slowly lowered her fork as he leaned forward in his chair to pluck a raspberry from his plate and slip it into his mouth. She watched his lips consume the berry and a swell of heat rose below her waist. She'd had those lips on her skin before and couldn't help but wonder what they'd feel like on other parts of her skin. She flushed with desire at the images even her innocent mind seemed to conjure. His mouth upon her breast, teeth scraping over a sensitive peak while his fingers played between her legs…

"Here let me…" he said, taking another raspberry and holding it out to her. She leaned forward, her lips parting to take the fruit from his fingers. The pads of his fingertips lingered at her mouth for a long moment before she moved back. Helen took another berry and held it out to him, eager to return the intimate gesture.

Gareth's lips took the fruit, but he caught her hand before it could retreat. He sucked the raspberry juice from her fingertips. The feel of his tongue on her fingers drew a soft sigh of pleasure from her as her body flamed to life. He continued to hold her wrist as he sucked each of her fingers, one at time, into his mouth. The look of satisfaction and hunger mixing on his face only made her hotter. It was as though he loved the taste of the berry juices on her skin and nothing was more satisfying than licking it from her flesh.

"Come closer to me."

Helen slid her chair over to his and he leaned into her, offering another raspberry. Only this time, as she swallowed it, he ducked his head and licked a wicked line up her neck and nibbled her ear. He leaned deeper into her, curling one arm around her waist as he embraced her. The combined sensations of swallowing sweetness and the feel of his hot tongue dancing up her throat lit a fire between her legs. A heavy, sharp ache slashed between her thighs, shooting upward. The sensation was almost painful and she couldn't bear it another second. Instinctively, she tried to pull away, to restore some control to herself, but his grasp on her waist wouldn't let her move. Gareth offered another berry. She took it almost greedily, and again he laved her throat, this time nipping her below her ear. A stinging shiver shot straight down her spine like she'd been struck by lightning. The hairs on the back of her neck and arms rose, and she trembled with the force of her heightened arousal. Helen couldn't breathe. Wetness pooled between her legs, and she started to shake. If he did that again, she'd lose her mind and her body.

Gareth released her hand and stood up.

"Should we retire to the drawing room?"

Helen managed a nod and took his offered arm. There were no servants in the halls as they walked, but someone had come in and lit a fire in the fireplace. There were two chairs and a loveseat. Helen watched Gareth for a clue as to where she should sit. He sat down on the loveseat, removing his black waistcoat. His white shirt molded to his muscles as he moved. She watched, desperate to see the skin beneath the shirt and feel the muscles move beneath her palms. What would it be like to put her hands to his flesh? To touch the source of such pleasure, such erotic sin, that she could scarcely breathe or think?

Gareth caught her staring and put his hand on the empty part of the seat next to him, patting it once. His silent command was clear. Helen knew she should have chosen the nearest chair. But damn the man, she wanted to be near him, to touch him, to let him touch her. She was quite close to begging him to make love to her. The ache was stronger every minute she spent in his presence.

Helen sat down on the edge of the loveseat, her hands clinging to her shawl as though it would give her strength. As though sensing her use of the fabric as a shield, Gareth reached out to her shoulder, coiling his fingers into the silk shawl. He slowly pulled it away from her, and she felt every inch of the cloth as it slid over the bare skin of her upper back. He dropped the shawl to the floor, out of reach, and then slid a few inches closer, gazing deeply into her eyes.

"Ask me..." he breathed.

One of his hands drifted down her back while the other hand alighted upon her knee, sliding slowly up her leg. Gareth's brown eyes were as warm as honey, yet they glinted with a dark lust that she had no power to resist.

"Ask me, Helen..." he urged. She knew what he wanted her to say.

"Please..." she whispered, not able to ask for more as she leaned in to kiss him. His fingers on her thigh slid higher as their lips met. His hand on her back pulled her closer, their knees touching. His lips caressed hers in the faintest echo of a kiss before he drew back.

"Not here... Come with me." He pulled her off the loveseat and back into the hall.

They ascended the stairs together and Helen

couldn't help but sense the inevitability of her situation. Tonight Gareth would possess her, body and soul, and she would not resist. She had to know how deep her passion for him ran. It was a dangerous question, but one that needed an answer.

She slowed as they passed her bedchamber, but he kept walking. At the end of the hall, he opened a door to another bedroom. It had to be his. There was an expansive four-poster bed, much bigger than the one she'd slept in. The sunlight weakened as dusk came in through the gauzy white curtains outlining the large windows. Gareth locked the door and faced her.

As he came towards her, the trembling started somewhere in her chest and spread throughout her body. He took her hands, holding them for a few seconds and absorbing the trembling before guiding her hands to his waist. Tentatively, she helped him pull his shirt out from his pants and up over his head. The flex of muscles and the broad expanse of sun-kissed skin made her a little dizzy. She had never been this close to an unclothed man. She was in turn nervous and excited.

She felt better, being in control of him as he undressed. He raised her hands to his lips, kissing them before he put them on his chest. For a long moment, she let the heat of his chest warm her, feeling the steady beat of his heart. His fingers curled around her wrists, keeping her close and anchoring her to him. She grew braver, exploring the smooth masculine skin. His hands followed hers at first, as though silently guiding her, showing her where her touch pleased him the most. Every time she swept her fingers around his flat nipples, across his throat, or down the slope of his abdomen, his lashes would lower and his lips would part with a faint panting breath.

She was so consumed with stroking his chest and watching his muscles ripple that she barely noticed his hands unlacing the back of her gown until it dropped to the floor at her feet in a whisper of fabric against flesh. He tugged gently at the several layers of petticoats and lifted her out from the mass of undergarments.

She remained quiet, heart racing, as he loosened her stays and those, too, fell to her ankles. When she was down to nothing but a chemise, Gareth wrapped his hands around her waist, picked her up, and set her on the edge of the bed. His hands slid her stockings off and moved her chemise up inch by agonizing inch.

She started trembling again and found the courage to speak his name. "Gareth…"

He froze when she spoke, his bright eyes shining in the gloom. "Yes?" he whispered.

"I'm nervous…" she confessed as his hands started moving again, baring her legs completely.

"I would never harm you. How can I convince you?" He moved slowly between her legs so that he stood against the bed's edge, their hips close but not quite touching.

"Kiss me. I forget everything else when you kiss me."

"Your wish is my command," he murmured, then delved deeply into her mouth with his tongue.

Her fear slowly receded in the wake of his consuming kisses. She didn't notice that he had pushed her back and removed his breeches. His mouth never left hers. He eased himself down on top of her, and she wrapped her legs around him, molding herself to his shape. His kisses became feverous and distracting until his length started to slide into her wet, swollen flesh. Helen dug her nails into his back, the spasm of pain shocking her as something tore deep inside her. She wanted to cry, but Gareth's kisses softened, and she relaxed. The pain lessened and finally faded. A tension replaced it, a desperate ache that she'd never felt before. He needed to move harder, faster, to ease the need.

"Are you all right?" he asked, holding still above her.

She nodded jerkily. "Yes. It doesn't hurt as much now."

Helen moved beneath him, raising her hips, completely wanton and crazed with desire. His hands slid the chemise up and off her body, barely missing a second of her kisses. Her breasts pressed against his smooth, hard chest, and a tremulous sigh escaped her lips as he settled deeper into her body. It felt right, this union in the darkness and the rushed thrill of their hips meeting and withdrawing, the touch of limbs, and the caress of lips in forbidden places.

Gareth grew tighter inside her, his movements harder, and she matched his pace, yearning to release the tension coiling in her own body. They came together, his eyes locking upon hers as their passion crested like a mighty wave. He relaxed into her as a flare of heat spread deep inside her. She kissed his lips and cheek, murmuring his name over and over again like a midnight prayer as pure joy shook her entire body. He opened his mouth as though to speak but seemed to change his mind and kissed her again. When he regained his strength, he eased off her but pulled her to him, cradling her in his arms. Even with the press of his warm body against hers, she shivered.

"Are you hurting?" He stroked her arm, trailing his fingertips down over one of her breasts. Her skin burned as he teased the soft curve of her hip and let his hand rest on her thigh.

"No… I'm just a little cold," she whispered back.

He chuckled and moved away, pulling the covers back onto the bed so they could slide between the sheets. "Better?"

"Much better." She rolled onto her side to face him. He was a dark silhouette against the moonlit windows behind him. Gareth brushed a lock of her hair back from her face, his thumb tracing her lower lip. She felt safe, content… Nothing in the world could ever harm her, not so long as he touched her, held her close. Helen drifted to sleep beneath his protective embrace.

Gareth watched her eyelids fall shut and listened to her soft steady breath as she drifted to sleep. She was so trusting, to give him her virginity, knowing it should have gone to the man she would have married. It was a gift, one he vowed to cherish. He smoothed a hand down the flair of her full hips, perfect for him to hold. It felt incredible to hold a woman in his arms, and not just any woman, but Helen. There was something irresistible about her that kept drawing him in like a moth to a flame.

At last he had found the contentment he'd been robbed of. The years he'd wasted looking in all the wrong places. One simple night with Helen had cleansed his heart. In her little sighs, shivers, and kisses, he'd been reborn. It reminded him of his time with Clarissa. Theirs had been a love match—a powerful one. They had played and romped about as children, quarreled as lovers, and united as man and wife.

Apart from his best friend, Ambrose Worthing, there had been no other person in his life he had trusted himself to love. But with Helen, he could feel that giddy rush of first passion and knew it could all too easily strengthen into deep love. It was dangerous to care for her as he did, but there could be no denying his feelings.

Could he marry her? He'd believed it wasn't possible, but he had ruined her, despite knowing he should not have touched her or kissed her. He'd gone and taken everything she could give and still wanted more. Gareth started to smile at the idea of marriage, but his smile wilted. He did not deserve Helen. She ought to have been courted properly by some strapping young lad who would write sonnets about her cornflower blue eyes and the tinkling bell of her laugh.

What could he offer her? An empty home, a wasted life, and a husband who was afraid to love? A woman often believed she loved the first man who showed her passion, but she might not love him. Could she come to love him in time? If he were to convince her to wed him? Would it be enough? If they married, would their union withstand being born as a ruthless transaction? Her virtue for his honor?

CHAPTER FOUR

Helen woke up to the light patter of rain against the windows. The bed was cold and empty beside her. She shivered, pulling the sheets tighter against her naked body. If only Gareth would come back to bed so she could wrap herself around his warm, hard body. She was deeply sore from the night before, but she still wanted to touch him, to share again the familiarity of his body in the way intimacy between lovers always came. A rush of heat flooded her as she remembered what Gareth had done to her, what she'd wanted him to do to her.

And now that she'd succumbed, the bed was empty. He had lost interest in her already. Helen bit her lip and tears welled up in her eyes. How could she go from crying over being stuck here to crying at the thought of having to leave? Men were disastrous to a woman's thought process. She'd have to avoid them in the future if she meant to think logically.

As she was steeling her nerves and deciding what she must do, the bedroom door opened. Gareth came in, fully dressed and carrying a tray with tea and scones, looking the picture of a country gentleman at his leisure. The brooding rake from the night before was gone, and in his place was a man more suited to happiness. The frown lines about his face had turned to laugh lines. Was he happy to be rid of her? Was he delighted that he'd had his fun and now would send her on her way? Part of her thought her panicked reaction was foolish, but she couldn't help it. She'd given herself to him and now she didn't know where she stood with him. Where did they go from here? He saw her watching him, and set the tray down to rush over to her.

"What's wrong, my darling?" He cupped her face and wiped her tears away.

He offered her comfort and sweetness, all the things she'd believed seconds before he was incapable of giving her. She really was a fool.

Helen tried to smile, looking at him through tear coated lashes. "I thought…oh, it doesn't matter."

"I brought you breakfast." He fetched the tray and joined her on the bed.

At first, Helen thought she was too ill to eat, but her appetite crept back and she nibbled on a currant scone. He hadn't abandoned her. Why the thought of him leaving her hurt, she wouldn't admit.

"Is everything well, Helen? Do you…hurt much?"

No eyes had ever looked at her that way, as

though she was the world and nothing beyond her existed. It made the budding warmth in her chest spread and deepen, erasing the chill of waking in his bed alone.

"It still hurts a little," she said, surprised that she could be so frank with him about such an embarrassing matter. But after last night, he knew her as no other man had. Hiding anything at this point seemed silly.

"It should pass. The next time it will hurt less," he promised.

She blushed at the idea of there being a next time. She was secretly glad to hear that. He would not send her away so soon then. Her gaze danced over his body…the way his breeches were snug on his muscular thighs and his silver waistcoat with embroidered thistle flowers made his eyes sparkle. He was the sort of man a woman would always want, in her bed, by her side. Handsome enough to make a woman's heart skitter and charming enough to steal her breath. Despite her soreness, she would gladly have fallen back in bed and rumpled the sheets further.

He seemed to read her thoughts and winked at her. "I'll leave you to eat. I have some letters to write. When you're feeling better…well…we'll find something to do." He flashed a rakish grin, kissed her forehead, and left her alone in his big empty bed.

Gareth lounged back in his chair, watching Ambrose pace before him. After he'd left Helen, he'd answered his letters and then Mary had found him, telling him Ambrose had come. His friend was now wearing a path into the carpet in front of Gareth's desk.

"What is it, Ambrose? I trust that Bennett fellow is well? I didn't hit the man that hard."

Ambrose's fists clenched and unclenched, a habit Gareth recognized from their youth. Ambrose was disturbed.

"Mr. Bennett is fine, a nasty bruise or two, but fine. It is Miss Banks that concerns me. I have only just been able to track down her brother."

Gareth felt the bottom of his stomach pitch out from under him. "You didn't tell him where Helen is, did you?" She couldn't leave now, he wasn't ready to let her go.

"No, I was not so foolish. Besides, he didn't even know me. He was on his way to Bennett's chambers, hoping to find him. I don't doubt that Bennett will tell Banks everything. You ought to be ready. Banks will either kill you or demand you marry his sister."

"And if I marry her?" Gareth replied.

Ambrose laughed darkly. "Come now, Gareth. We both know you swore you would never marry again. No one could ever compare to Clarissa. She was your other half."

He would have agreed with Ambrose years ago, but now that he'd met Helen, he knew a happy life with someone other than Clarissa was possible again. Salvation was within reach—actually, in his bed at this moment. The mental image of that was too hard to resist. He smiled.

"Why are you smiling?" Ambrose demanded.

"I suppose it's because I'm happy," he admitted, still grinning.

His friend stopped pacing and crossed his arms over his chest, glaring down at Gareth. "I know the proper course is marriage, but Gareth, you can't marry her. Miss Banks deserves someone…"

"Better?"

Ambrose laughed. "I was going to say someone less jaded."

"And you think I cannot give Helen what she needs?"

Gareth's friend, looking troubled, leaned one elbow against the wall across from the desk. "I think it has been a long time since either of us has been in the position to offer a woman what she needs, aside from physical pleasure."

"I can offer her a home, food, clothes… It's more than she has the ability to get now. Her brother has lost the last of their money. I've compromised her, and she'll never be able to gain a position as a governess. It's the least I can do, and what's more, I *want* to marry her."

"Want or not, you cannot. She deserves a green lad who will adore her every word and bring her flowers every day. Not someone like you or me. We're not made for marriage."

Gareth's heart turned over in his chest. He wanted to give Helen more than just pleasure. He wanted to care for her, protect her the way her brother had failed to do. But she deserved better than him. The last seven years of his life had been absolutely horrible. It was his own fault, of course. He'd chosen that path of degradation. Could he bring her into that life, with his reputation for gaming and now dueling? What could he truly offer her besides a man jaded by life and ruined for love?

"As always, you are right, Ambrose. I cannot marry her."

After breakfast, Helen returned to her chambers and bathed in a small tub. She washed herself, careful to be gentle on certain parts of her body. The tenderness was welcome, though, as was the change she felt deep inside her. She was privy to a secret understanding about herself as a woman and what mysteries her body held when in the arms of a man. There was something more, though…a deeper sense of wholeness she hadn't felt before, like being loved… Was she loved by Gareth? Smiling, she walked over to the bed where a bright summer green gown with gold ribbons on the sleeves and hem was laid out. Mary helped her dress.

"Where is Mr. Fairfax?" Helen asked Mary.

Mary's face darkened, her lips pursed into a thin line. "He's in his study, down the hall past the library." The way Mary said this made Helen's stomach churn unpleasantly.

"Am I allowed to see him?" she asked quietly.

"I suppose. He gave me no instruction that he was not to be disturbed."

"Thank you, Mary." Helen kissed Mary's cheek lightly and darted out of her room. She passed the tall grandfather clock in the hall on the way to Gareth's study. It was nearly noon. Her slippered feet made no sound on the wood floor as she approached the open study door. A pair of masculine voices drifted down to her. Helen crept across the hallway to lean against the wall next to the door, eavesdropping.

"As always, you are right, Ambrose. I cannot marry her." Gareth sighed heavily.

"I knew you would understand. Well, I must return to Bath, but come and find me when you have returned Miss Banks to her brother."

Helen scrambled away from the doorway and ducked around the corner, avoiding Mr. Worthing as he passed by. When he was gone, Helen exhaled slowly, her body shaking as she absorbed the depth of Gareth's words. He was sending her home. He didn't want her. Well, if he was going to treat her that way, she wouldn't stay here anyway. She squared her shoulders and walked into his study.

Gareth was sitting at his desk when she came in. He glanced up briefly, the look momentarily soft before it sharpened and cooled.

"Ahh Miss Banks, I'm glad you're here." His tone and manner were all wrong. He hadn't called her *Helen*. A heavy stone hit the pit of her stomach, echoing hard and painful. She placed a hand on her abdomen as a wave of nausea hit her like a physical blow. His coldness was more cutting and crueler than anything she could have imagined. She wanted to say his name, remind him of what they had shared. But she knew it wouldn't matter.

"My coach will take you home tomorrow morning. I will speak to Mary. She can arrange for your new clothes and other items to return to Bath with you."

The world began to fade at the edges, and a sharp ringing clouded Helen's ears. She had never been the sort of woman who fainted, but at the moment, she felt perilously close to it. She knew what he was going to do, but hearing him say it hurt like nothing before had in her entire life. Helen stumbled to a nearby chair and collapsed into it. Gareth started to come over to her, but she waved him away.

"Please, do not trouble yourself." She managed a few deep, slow breaths, mastering herself. This should be no worse than the duel...but it was, because death would have ended her fear. Now, the panic and pain would subside into an aching despair once he sent her away. She wasn't sure how long she sat slumped in the chair before she found the energy to move. Helen stood up and looked him in the eye. How right he'd been to say love was pain. Now she understood. To love was to hurt.

"Thank you, sir, for your kindness. But I shall not trouble you further. I will not take a thing from this house which I did not bring with me. Our arrangement was the settlement of my brother's debt. I see that after last night, you feel I have paid that account in full." She wanted to demand that he ready the coach now. She wanted to scream, to yell, but her heart was breaking. She could almost hear it shattering like glass on stone.

She loved him. *She loved Gareth Fairfax.* The cold-hearted duelist had seduced her. She'd lost her virginity, her heart, and her hope in only one day as a prisoner of his paradise. The sooner she left, the better. Time would be the only remedy available to heal her, and with a sinking feeling, she worried it wouldn't be enough.

His eyes flashed with fire. "I insist you take the clothing. They would be of no use to me."

Shame tore through her at his words. She lashed out. "Wouldn't they?" Let him give his next woman her clothes. She couldn't bear to feel the silks on her skin and think of him. No, she needed never to touch them ever again.

"Just what are you implying, Helen?" Her name on his lips only fanned the flames of her anger further. *Now* he would call her by her name? Her hands fisted at her sides as she fought to stay in control of her sudden flare of temper. It bit at her inside like a vicious dog.

"I think you know exactly what I'm implying," she shot back.

His face was turning a dark red with anger. "I know you need more clothes, and I want you to take them!" he snapped.

"How dare you pity me? How dare you!" she shouted, her voice sharp with hurt and anger. Her entire body was shaking with rage.

"Pity?" He marched over to her, glowering at her, but confusion lit his eyes.

"What else could it be but pity? You've stolen the only thing I had left, my dignity. No man will touch me now. You've ruined me." She was venomous, harsh, and cruel, but she had to protect herself. If there was one thing she'd learned in the past several months, it was that no one else would ever take care of her besides herself.

He made as though to grab her, but she jumped back and fled the room. Tears blurred her eyes as she ran down the hall and out into the gardens. She tripped over a low cut rose bush but caught herself before falling and hurried to the garden gate. Her left ankle stung and her skirts were torn from the thorns but she didn't stop. The rain pelted her skin, cold and thick, as it started to soak through her clothes. Above her, the skies were lowering with heavy rain. The deep blue of the clouds was dark and ominous, a fair reflection of her ravaged soul. Her heart thundered against her breast as though trying in vain to escape the crushing despair of her body as she struggled through the archway. Again she was caught by the momentary spell of leaving Gareth's world to enter the wild, untamed land beyond. A distant growl from the sky heralded a deepening of the storm, but she didn't care.

Let it pour, let it drown me. I don't care anymore... It was a devastating truth for her to realize that the reason she drew breath existed no longer. How did one recover from such a shock to the heart and soul? The chill of the water on her skin was icy, and a shudder racked her as she forced herself to keep moving.

"Helen!" Gareth was at the door of the house, calling after her.

She darted into the meadow. Her gown hung heavy as the hemline absorbed the water from the high grass. The thick blades whipped and stung her skin through the waterlogged gown that clung to her shins. She paused only a second to get her bearings. The sloping hills were a pale gold brown with the heavy rain and dark gray clouds hung low in the sky.

"Helen, wait!" Gareth shouted again. He was closer, but she didn't look back.

She started running, pulling her gown up above her knees as she tore through the grass. Thunder rumbled, the earth vibrating with its fury. She was halfway through the meadow when Gareth caught up with her. He lunged for her, catching her at an awkward angle, and they both fell. He rolled, taking the brunt of the fall as they went down before he moved and put her beneath him. Helen was trapped, his arms and legs pinning her down. His face was dark with his fury, his brown eyes shadowed with desperation.

"Let go of me!" She strained to hit him.

"No." His tone was hard, edged with desperation.

She felt his hard length against the wet fabric of her gown, and even in her anger, she still wanted him. Helen freed one arm and tried to hit him again, he caught her wrist and trapped it at her side. The cold, wet grass shifted beneath her as he moved fully on top of her. His free hand dug at her gown, pushing it up. She squirmed, her legs trying to kick out, but his knees forced her legs apart.

"Don't you dare!" She clawed at his chest, but he wasn't going to stop. His mouth sought hers, but she turned her head away in defiance. If he kissed her, she'd give in and make love to him. His lips fell to her neck, rough and hot as he sucked on her skin. She felt his hands bunching up her petticoats.

"Tell me you don't want me, and I'll stop," he growled.

"I…" she weakened beneath him, wanting him no matter how furious she was with him.

Gareth rubbed his hips against hers, and with one hand, he loosened his trousers.

"Go on, Helen. Tell me what it is you really want," he purred, freeing her trapped wrists.

She bit her lip so hard she drew blood and then started tearing at his clothes, desperate to get closer to him, to feel his hot skin on her own cold flesh.

"You. I want you," she ground out.

Gareth didn't wait a second longer, he pushed his way inside, taking her, claiming her, and she gloried in the soreness mingling with her aching desire.

Helen arched her back, taking him in deeper with a low moan, unable to prevent anything else. Her eyes burned with tears as she fought her feelings for him. How could she yearn to stay with him when she would never mean anything more to him than this? Yet she was determined to enjoy these last few minutes with him, feeling alive for the last time in a way she knew she'd never feel again.

The rain fell harder and harder, the thundering skies responding to Gareth's savage possession of her. As her body quaked in reaction to him, she stopped caring that he was using her. She would use him back. She turned her head, her one free hand catching his chin and pulling his mouth to hers. He grunted against her lips, adjusting himself as he thrust even harder into her. Their bodies moved together in a frantic symphony of sighs, sliding limbs, and whispered words of encouragement. One of his hands slid down to her bare thigh, slick with rain. His fingers dug into her skin as he pulled her leg tighter against his hip. Their heavy breaths and harsh grinding merged as they climaxed.

Gareth gasped loudly as he came inside her. She continued to move beneath him, taking her pleasure for a moment longer before her body shuddered along with his. He kept her trapped beneath him. She would not escape again, not yet. Her head fell back into the grass, wet strands of her gold hair spilling out around her. Her breasts rose and fell with her heavy breathing. Gareth saw the two tempting peaks beneath the wet gown and nearly came a second time, wishing he could see them as he had last night. He rocked back slowly, still fully inside her.

A flicker of guilt shot through him. He

shouldn't have done this—not so soon and not after he'd resolved to send her away. Finally, he forced himself to pull out, rolling over onto the grass next to her as he fixed his trousers. Her creamy white legs shook, raindrops coating her bared limbs. A few small scrapes marred one of her ankles.

"You're hurt," he murmured, reaching for her ankle. He wanted to cuddle her into his lap and carry her back to the safety of his bed where he could tend to her cuts.

"I'm fine." She jerked out of his hold, refusing to glance his way.

He watched as she tried to fix her torn petticoats and pull her gown down. She sat up, her entire body vibrating as her eyes looked straight ahead at the sloping hills in the distance.

She wiped tears and raindrops from her cheeks. Her face, once so open and easy to read, closed up like a castle's portcullis dropping down, the heavy iron sinking deep into the soil, sealing him outside forever. The passion they'd recaptured was slipping away, and there was nothing he could do to stop it. He was losing her—truly losing her—and it scared him out of his mind. With Clarissa, God had taken her. But Helen was leaving because he was a damned coward and a fool.

Without looking at him, she stood up, wobbling once before she spoke.

"I will be gone from here as soon as Mary can have the coach ready. Do not attempt to stop me." Her last words were cold and firm. He did not want to know where she could find such coldness within herself. He hadn't thought her capable of it. Maybe his mercenary treatment had put it there. By sending her away, doing what was best for her, he had turned her cold, just like himself. The thought left a bitter sting in his mouth.

Gareth didn't respond. He let her walk away, but his eyes followed her hungrily, desperately memorizing the curves of her breasts and hips, so clearly outlined by her drenched gown. He bowed his head as he forced his thoughts elsewhere to ease the pang of his breaking heart and the renewed lust in his groin. There was no crueler torture than loving and wanting a woman he could not have. He dared not get up until she was well out of sight, back in the safety of the gardens, so he would not be tempted to make love to her again. By the time he made it back to the house, he saw not a single servant except Mary. The moment he stepped inside to escape the rain, she was there, glaring at him.

"Don't look at me like that," he growled.

She continued to glare, her gray eyes throwing daggers. "There is a gentleman in the parlor. He wishes to speak with you."

"Gentleman? What gentleman?"

"He would not give his name sir, but he and Miss Banks are two sides of a coin if I ever saw one," Mary declared.

Gareth's stomach clenched in irritating knots. Of course Martin Banks would choose now to show up and rescue Helen.

"I'll see to him directly. Thank you, Mary." He growled and left her standing by the door, no doubt still scowling at his backside. He didn't bother to change into dry clothes, he was too tired and frustrated to care about his appearance. He burst into the parlor, sending the door crashing loudly into the wall.

"Banks?" he snapped. He wanted to be done with this, to put distance and time between himself and this awful situation. The room seemed to be empty. He turned around, finding himself face-to-face with Helen's twin brother, a cocked pistol aimed at his chest.

He wasn't afraid. Martin would either pull the trigger or he wouldn't. Gareth was already dead inside. Losing Helen had destroyed him.

"Where is my sister?" Martin, a man Gareth had sworn could care less about Helen, now had a heroic glow of determination in his handsome face. Gareth saw his eyes were just like Helen's, his nose and lips were so like hers yet more masculine where hers had been delicate and feminine. They were truly as Mary had said, "two sides of a coin". It would be hard to deal with this man when all Gareth saw was Helen in his every feature.

"Where is she, Fairfax? I know she's here." Martin's finger tightened slightly on the trigger.

"She's probably in her chamber, packing her things. She is leaving."

"You're damned right she is." Martin shoved Gareth into one of the tall-backed chairs and bent down over him. "I ought to blow you to hell for what you've done to her." Martin's voice was soft but black with hate. "You've compromised my sister. She should have been able to make a good match or find a post as a governess. But no! You took advantage of a sweet and caring woman whose only weakness was her kindness. You're a damned bastard, and I will see you dead over this." He jammed the muzzle of his pistol into Gareth's chest, his hand shaking slightly with his anger.

"What about you, you coward? She fought your duel for you, even managed to graze my bloody arm. You're lucky she gave herself away before I decided to fire my shot. And need I tell you that you've done a poor job of caring for her?"

"What the devil do you mean?" Martin spat viciously.

Gareth plowed ahead, anger emanating from him.

"When I brought her here, it became immediately clear that the girl was half starved and had no proper clothes. To my horror, I discovered she'd been abstaining from food to feed you, and that the two of you were barely getting by. It was your duty to care for her. Family should mean something to you." Gareth delivered his verbal blow to a stunning effect. Martin's pistol lowered half an inch as he processed Gareth's words.

"Was my duty?" Martin replied suspiciously.

"I've compromised your sister. I mean to rectify the situation however I can. I want to keep her safe and cared for. If I thought I deserved her, I'd marry her, but I don't. She's too good a woman for me, but I'll be damned if I don't make sure she's goes without food or decent clothes again." He meant it with every violent beat of his heart and ragged breath as he faced her brother down.

"Helen doesn't need you."

Gareth's gaze was thunderous. "She may not need me, but she certainly doesn't need you, either. You're starving her and running her into the ground with your gambling. If she'll let me, I can give her the life a woman like her deserves."

"She's not going to marry you. Helen would only marry a man who loved her." Martin didn't even flinch at Gareth's blazing glare.

"I love her enough that losing her will drive me mad, but I know she won't have me. And I've destroyed her future and will do what I can to make amends. There can only be me or spinsterhood, and given your proclivity to gamble, she will likely be dead from starvation in a fortnight if left with you."

Before either man could speak further, Helen materialized between them. The look of hurt and betrayal in her eyes made his blood freeze in his veins. Shame flamed his face and he looked away for a brief instant.

"Helen..." Gareth started, but the words withered on his lips as he saw her. An agonizing maelstrom of dark emotions played across her face. It struck him numb with dread. She'd heard what he'd said, that she was destroyed and her brother couldn't care for her. The damned fool didn't even handle his sister being compromised properly. The Banks twins were a disaster if left to take care of themselves.

Helen forced her brother's pistol to point down at the carpet. "Martin, we are leaving. *Now*." Helen's voice was different, harder. Her brother didn't argue. He let her pull him away from Gareth, who made no move to follow. He remained in his chair, listening to the rumble of thunder from both the skies and within his soul.

CHAPTER FIVE

Helen and her brother rode down the muddy lane away from Gareth's house. The horses kicked up puddles, and for a long while, the only sound was the splashing and the patter of rain.

She'd donned her brother's stolen clothes once more, wanting to take only what she'd brought. Helen had no need for Gareth's charity. Mary had insisted they take a pair of Gareth's horses, with instructions on how to return them once they'd reached Bath.

"How did you find me, Martin?"

Martin's cheeks reddened as though embarrassed. "After I had the maid pick the lock on my door, I found my extra breeches and overcoat were missing. I was ready to panic when I received a note from Rodney Bennett. I went to see him immediately, and he told me everything about the duel. It seems he felt responsible for you falling into Fairfax's clutches. The hard part was finding Fairfax's house. I had to walk the second half here after I got a ride from a farmer in his cart."

Helen didn't say anything for a long while, just rode in silence. She didn't want to think about Martin or what they were going to do when they got back to Bath. All she could think about was Gareth—his smile, his touch, the sweet way he kissed her, and the passionate way he showed her how close a man and woman could be. The union of bodies and souls, when all time seemed to slow and nothing was stronger than the shared breathing and the locked gazes. There was a holiness to that moment, a sacred spell woven between the lovers' hearts that could never be undone. No matter what harsh words one might say or the cruel actions one might do, a person was bound forever in the depth of that connection, unable to escape the pull. She was no different.

Martin tugged the reins of his horse, bringing it closer to hers. "Helen... Was it true, what he said?"

"About what?" She struggled to focus on her brother.

"The food...and the clothes." His mouth pulled into a grim line.

She was tired of pretending that everything was fine, that life was good. Martin's decisions had cost her too much.

"Yes, it's true."

"Why didn't you tell me? I would have..."

"You would have what? Gambled harder? Lost me to another man? No thank you. I've paid your debt to Gareth and it stops here." She vowed resolutely. Things were going to be different now. She was not going to let Martin control their future. He'd had his chance and she'd suffered long enough.

"How did you pay him?" Martin's voice was hoarse, as though he was afraid he already knew the answer.

"He was very lonely. You see… He lost his wife and child. In exchange for your life, I stayed at his house and kept him company. I was his companion." She felt strangely compelled to justify his actions. She understood him, after all…his unhappiness was from his loneliness.

Martin's face paled. "Companion? You mean he actually…"

"Yes, I was *that* sort of companion. He ruined me, as he put it." She did not spare him anything. After his lack of responsibility, it was time Martin understood what price she'd paid for him.

"I should have shot him," Martin cursed.

Helen flashed him a vicious look. "No, you shouldn't have. He was kind to me, more than kind. I wanted for nothing and…" Helen stopped before she said something she'd regret.

"And?" Martin prompted, his eyes suddenly sharp, seeing something in her reaction that she hadn't meant to betray. "Don't tell me you fell in love with him." Martin stared at her.

Helen blushed, more from anger at herself than anything else. "It wouldn't matter if I did. He didn't want me. He let me go."

"Helen, the man only let you leave because I had

a pistol on him. Bullets can be very persuasive. He cares for you—" Her brother's features were blurred with confusion, as though he was sorting something out in his mind.

"He doesn't."

"How do you know?"

"Because I do," Helen snapped. There would be no way to unhear the words he'd spoken in his study when speaking with Ambrose. He'd never marry her. If he loved her, marriage wouldn't have been a problem. It was that simple.

"Well, you didn't see his face when he was lecturing me on how I failed you. He loves you. He practically shouted at me that he loved you. I may be terrible at cards, but I'd wager my very life that he would marry you if he thought he deserved you. If you love him, I won't stand in the way."

Martin stopped his horse abruptly, forcing Helen to do the same. The skies shook with distant thunder.

"Hurry, Martin. We've a long way to go before nightfall." Helen's response held a note of irritation.

"Helen, perhaps you should go back to him. If he loves you...and you love him...well, it's that simple isn't it? I'd rather you were safe and happy, that you were *loved*, than suffering with me."

Since when had he ever given her happiness a second thought?

"I'm serious, Helen. At least think about it. I saw his face. He cares deeply for you. How can you turn your back on that?"

She peeped up at him from under her lashes. For the first time in years, she felt that old connection to him, as twins, return to her. He was thinking of her again, about how she felt. He hadn't done that in a long time. It made her consider his words more carefully. Could she return to Gareth? Would he take her back if she threw herself upon his mercy? Did he care enough about her that they could make a go of it? Did he truly love her?

"What about you?" she asked softly. If she returned to Gareth, she'd be leaving Martin to fend for himself.

Her brother flashed her a winning smile. "I'll get by. It is time I took care of myself."

Helen stared at him for a long time, wondering if he could. His face was solemn and his eyes were hard with determination, a look she'd never seen before. Had her leaving him changed him for the better? Perhaps he realized she was not a crutch he could lean on.

"I mean it. I am done with the gambling hells. I'll apply for clerkship positions with some of the local barristers starting first thing tomorrow. Father still has a few friends here, and I know which men to call upon for employment."

The tightness in her chest eased and she knew he meant it. Martin would be fine, and she could be with Gareth. Everything would be all right. It had to be. She would fight for her happiness and Gareth's.

Finally, she turned her horse back to face Gareth's home—her home—if he would still have her.

"What the devil are you waiting for? Go back to him!" Martin reached forward and whapped her horse's flank with his crop. The horse jumped into a slow gallop back down the road. Helen clung to the reins and dug her heels into the stirrups to remain astride.

By the time she reached the house, she was soaked to the bone. A groomsman ran out to catch her horse's reins and help her down. She breathed a quick thank you to him and went inside. Mary, lecturing a servant on tracking mud through the house, froze when she saw Helen.

"Where is he?" Helen asked her.

"In the garden. Determined to catch his death in this weather. He was muttering about climbing trees. I couldn't stop him. He's in one of his moods," Mary replied grimly.

Helen headed toward the door to the gardens. Through the small window, she caught a glimpse of a pair of fine legs in black trousers vanishing up between the branches of a tree. Helen opened the door and strode out to the tree, trying to figure out what she was going to say.

She looked up to see him resting on a familiar branch, his eyes gazing into the distance. He didn't seem to hear her approach. She waited a long moment, burning him into her memory in case he sent her away again. His shirt was wet and clung to his muscles, their fine lines so vivid in her memory that her body shivered at the ghost of lost passion. Gareth's hair was nearly black with the rain as it curled slightly at the ends.

"Shall I have the head gardener fetch you a ladder, Master Gareth?" She mimicked Mary's voice.

"No Mary, that won't be nec…" His head dropped as he peered down at her. His eyes were wide, his lips parted as though stunned to see her.

"Helen?" He scrambled quickly back down the branches, sending a storm of leaves around her head. He dropped to the ground in front of her.

Helen's momentary coyness evaporated. She felt a wave of desperation to beg him to let her stay.

"What are you doing here?" He sucked in a breath.

"I had to come back…" When he didn't say anything, she wondered if she had to justify her staying. "I could work for you. I can be a maid… whatever you want. It doesn't matter, just let me stay. I'll earn my keep." Helen tried to make her voice steadier, but she still sounded terribly desperate.

"Earn your keep?" Gareth looked like he was trying not to laugh.

Helen's eyes burned with tears of shame. "I can learn to clean. I may not be good at it, but I'm sure that Mary could teach me the proper way." Helen started to reach for him but stopped and wrapped her arms around herself instead.

"Please, Gareth…" One brave tear fell down her check, and all the merriment in his eyes died.

He took two slow steps toward her, cupping her face in his hands as he gazed into her eyes. "I won't let you stay on as a servant, Helen. You could never be a maid."

"But…" Her voice constricted with panic, but he silenced her with his lips.

He kissed her in a strange mix of fierce passion

and aching emotion. He had never kissed her this way before. It felt like the first time he'd kissed her in the drawing room, yet it seared with the passion of the meadow and warmed her soul like when he'd first made love to her. It was a kiss that would never end, a promise that they would remain this way forever. When he finally freed her lips, he rested his forehead against hers, keeping them close.

"Stay here because you love me, because you'll make me happy again," he whispered.

"I will, even if you don't love me. If you care enough to want me even a little, I'll stay."

"Care for you? Helen, I not only care for you, I love you. I want to marry you, if you'll have me, the black-hearted monster that I am."

"You want to marry me?" It couldn't be true, he couldn't love her that much… The idea was too wonderful to be true.

"Will you marry me, Helen?" Gareth's hands slid from her face down to her shoulders.

"Of course!" She stood up on tiptoe to kiss him. He happily obliged.

"Could Martin visit us?" she gasped suddenly, remembering her brother and how he and Gareth hadn't been friendly towards each other.

"Devil take it," Gareth muttered. "As long as he stays clear of the card tables, he is welcome to visit or even stay here. There is plenty of room, and he'd be one more person for Mary to happily fret over. Perhaps I can offer him a better example of how a gentleman should conduct himself. It is time he learned."

"You would do that?" Helen's brows rose in astonishment.

"For you, I would do anything." The husky timbre of his voice had her trembling. His words rocked her to her very core. It was the words she'd always longed to hear from a man she'd someday hoped would love her. She trembled in his arms, overcome with awe of his love and hers.

"We should get inside before we freeze," Gareth said, aware of Helen shivering in his arms. He wrapped his right arm about her waist and they began the short walk back to the house. He paused as they reached the door.

"You know, we'll have to come up with a story as to how we met," he said pensively.

"You don't want to tell people that you blackmailed and seduced me over my brother's gambling debts?" Helen smiled devilishly at him.

"That, I would happily own up to. It is the part where my wife nearly kills me in a duel which is the most disturbing part of the tale." He grinned.

"But I rather liked that part! It makes me sound very brave."

"Y o u *were* brave, my darling." His laugh reverberated through her as he held her tight against his chest.

"Say that again," she begged.

"That you were brave?" He raised his eyebrows, his eyes crinkling with silent laughter.

"No, the other part," she breathed.

"My darling." His lips brushed hers in a fiery prelude to his kiss.

The Seduction continues…

An exclusive excerpt of *Wicked Designs*, The League of
Rogues Book 1
© Lauren Smith 2014 - Published by Samhain
Publishing

League Rule 4

When seducing a lady, any member of the League
may pursue her until she has declared her interest in a
particular member, and at such time, all pursuits of the
lady by others must cease.

Excerpt from *The Quizzing Glass Gazette*, April 3,
1820, The Lady Society Column:

*Lady Society was quite entertained earlier this week,
when she was witness to yet another wicked scheme
perpetuated by a member of London's notorious League of
Rogues. His Grace, the Duke of Essex, was seen to have been
seducing a most attractive widow in the midst of a musicale
hosted by Viscount Sheridan.*

*It seems the duke has truly broken with his long time
paramour Miss Evangeline Mirabeau. For all marriage
minded mamas, there is a collective sigh of sadness that His
Grace is a determined bachelor with no intent to marry.
Shame upon His Grace for not being a gentleman that
mothers could safely marry their daughters to and indulging
in his wicked lifestyle.*

*Lady Society will continue to watch the League with the
keenest interest…*

London, September 1820

Something wasn't right. Emily Parr allowed the elderly coachman to help her into the town coach, and the queer look he gave her made her skin crawl. Peering into the dark interior of the vehicle, she was surprised to find it empty. Uncle Albert was supposed to accompany her to social engagements and if not him, certainly a chaperone. Why then was the coach empty?

She settled into the back seat, her hands clutching her reticule tight enough that the beadwork dug into her palms through her gloves. Perhaps her uncle was meeting with his business partner, Mr. Blankenship. She'd seen Blankenship arrive just before she'd gone upstairs to prepare for the ball. A shudder rippled through her. The man was a lecherous creature with beetle-black eyes and hands that tended to wander too freely whenever he was near her. Emily was not worldly, having only just turned eighteen a few months earlier, but this last year with her uncle had enlightened her to a new side of life and none of it had been good.

Her first London Little Season should have been

a wonderful experience. Instead it had begun with the death of her parents at sea and ended with her new life in the dusty tomb of her uncle's townhouse. With an insubstantial library, no pianoforte and no friends, Emily had started to slide into a melancholy haze. It was crucial she make a good match and fast. She had to escape Uncle Albert's world, and the only way she could do that was to legally obtain her father's fortune.

A distant cousin of her mother's held the money in trust. It was a frustrating thing to have a man she'd never met hold the purse strings on her life. Uncle Albert despised the situation as well. As her guardian he was forced to give an accounting to her mother's cousin, which thankfully kept him from delving too deeply into her accounts for his own needs. The small fortune was the best bargaining chip she had to entice potential suitors. Though the money would go to her husband, she hoped to find a man who would respect her enough not to squander what was rightfully hers. But arriving at the ball without a chaperone would damage her chances in husband hunting, it simply wasn't done to show up alone. It spoke lowly of her uncle as well as their financial situation.

As relieved as she was to not have her uncle or Mr. Blankenship escorting her, her stomach still clenched. She recalled the cold way the elderly driver smiled at her just before she'd climbed inside. The slickness of that grin made her feel a little uneasy, like he knew something she didn't and it amused him. It was silly—the old man wasn't a threat. But she couldn't shake the wariness that rippled through her.

She would have been thankful for Uncle Albert's presence, even if it meant another lecture on how costly she was to provide for and how kind he'd been in taking her in after her parents' ship was lost.

The driver was engaged to bring her to Chessley House for the ball, and nothing would go wrong. If she kept saying it over and over, she might believe it. Emily focused her thoughts on what tonight would bring, hoping to ease her worry. She would join her new friend, Anne Chessley, as well as Mrs. Judith Pratchet, an old friend of Anne's mother, who'd kindly agreed to sponsor Emily for the Little Season. There was every possibility she would meet a man and catch his interest enough that he would approach her uncle for permission to court her.

Emily almost smiled. Perhaps tonight she would dance with the Earl of Pembroke.

Last night, the handsome earl had smiled at her during their introduction and asked her to dance. Emily had nearly wept with disappointment when she informed him that Mrs. Pratchet had already filled her dance card.

The earl had replied, "Another time, then?" and Emily nodded eagerly, hoping he would remember her.

Perhaps tonight I shall have a spot of luck. She desperately hoped so. Emily wasn't so foolish as to believe she had any real chance of marrying a man like the Earl of Pembroke, but it was nice to be noticed by a man of his standing. Sometimes that attention was noticed by others.

The coach halted sharply a moment later, and she

nearly toppled out of her seat, her thoughts interrupted, her daydreams fleeing.

"Ho there, my good man!" a man shouted from nearby.

Emily moved toward the door, but the vehicle rocked as someone climbed onto the driver's seat, and she fell back in her seat again.

"Twenty pounds is yours if you follow those two riders ahead and do as we ask," the newly-arrived man said.

Having regained control of her balance, she flung the coach curtains back. Two riders occupied the darkened street, their backs to her. What was going on? A sense of ill-ease settled deep in her stomach. The coach jerked and moved again. As she had feared, the driver didn't stop at Chessley House. He followed the riders ahead.

What was this? A kidnapping? A robbery? Should she stick her head out of the window and ask them to stop? If robbing her was their intent, asking them what they were doing might be a bad idea... Why would they take her when there were so many other heiresses, ones more lovely than her, having their first come out this year? Surely this wasn't an abduction. Her mind reeled as she struggled to cope with the situation. What would her father have done in this situation? Load a pistol and fight them off. Having no pistol, she'd have to think of something clever. Could these men be reasoned with? *Unlikely.*

Emily worried her bottom lip as she debated her options. She could scream for help, but such a reaction could worsen matters. She could open the door and throw herself out onto the street, but the clatter of hooves behind the coach erased that idea. She'd be lucky to survive the fall if she tried, and the horses behind were too close. She'd likely be killed. Emily fell back against the seat with a shaky sigh, her heart racing. She'd have to wait until the driver stopped.

For what seemed like an hour she kept nervously glancing out the windows to assess what direction the coach was going. By now London was far behind her. Only open country stretched on both sides of the road. A rumble of hooves heralded an approaching rider, and a man astride a sleek black gelding galloped past the window. He was too close and the horse too tall for her to get a good view of him. The moonlight rippled off the horse's shiny coat as it rode past.

She knew by the close proximity of the rider and the determined way he rode in the saddle that he was involved with this business. Who in their right mind, except perhaps that foul old man, Blankenship, would kidnap her? He'd be the sort to engage in such a nefarious activity.

The other evening he'd come to dinner at her uncle's house and when her uncle had turned away for only a second, Blankenship had twined one of this thick, stubby fingers around a lock of her hair, tugging it hard until she'd nearly cried out. He'd whispered horrible things in her ear, nasty things that made her sick as he told her he planned to marry her as soon as her uncle had approved. Emily had stared back at him, stating she'd never marry him. He'd only laughed and said, "We'll see, my sweet. We shall see."

Well, she wouldn't back down. She wasn't some pawn to be captured and held at someone's mercy. They'd have to fight to take her.

Emily looked out the window on the other side to count the riders. Two led the party at the front, mere yards ahead. Another two flanked the coach on either side. One of them rode with a second horse roped to his saddle, likely for the man who rode now with the driver. Not the best of odds. Perhaps she could outsmart them.

The coach slowed, then gently creaked to a stop. Emily took stock of her situation. She fought for composure, each breath slower than the one before. If she panicked, she might not survive. She had to hide. But she could not physically escape *five* men.

Her eyes fell to the seat across from her.

Maybe—

Godric St. Laurent, the twelfth Duke of Essex, leaned back in his saddle watching the abduction he'd orchestrated unfold. Covering his mouth with a gloved hand, he stifled a yawn. Things were going smoothly. In fact, this entire kidnapping bordered on the point of tedious. They'd intercepted the coach ten minutes before it reached Chessley House. No one witnessed the escort of riders or the driver changing his route. Oddly enough, the young woman hadn't shown any signs of resistance or concern from inside the coach. Wouldn't she have made some protestations when she realized what was happening? A thought stopped him dead. Had she somehow slipped out of the coach when they'd slowed on a corner before they'd left town? Surely not, they would have seen her. Most likely she was too terrified to do anything, hence the silence from inside. Not that she had anything to fear, she would not be harmed.

He nodded to his friend Charles who was perched next to the driver. A bag of coins jingled as Charles dropped it into the jarvey's waiting hands.

They had reached the halfway point between London and Godric's ancestral estate. They would go the rest of the way on horseback, with the girl sharing a horse with either him or one of his friends. The driver would return to London with a message for Albert Parr and a wild story that exonerated himself from blame.

"Ashton, stay here with me." Godric waved his friend over while the others rode the horses a good distance away to wait for his signal. Abductions were tricky things, and having only himself and one other man take hold of the girl would be better. She might have a fit of hysterics if she saw the other three men too close.

He rode up to the coach, curious to see whether the woman inside matched his memory. He'd seen her once before from a window overlooking the gardens when he'd visited her uncle. She'd been kneeling in the flowerbeds, her dress soiled as she weeded. A job more suited to a servant than a lady of quality. He'd been ready to dismiss her from his mind when she'd turned and glanced about the garden, a smudge of dirt on the tip of her upturned nose. A butterfly from a nearby flower had fluttered above her head. She hadn't noticed it, even as it settled on her long, coiling auburn hair. Something in his chest gave a funny little flip, and his body had stirred with desire. Any other woman so innocent would not have caught his interest, but he'd glimpsed a keenness in her eyes, a hidden intelligence as she dug into the soil. Miss Emily Parr was different. And different was intriguing.

Ashton handed the driver the ransom letter for Parr and took up a position near the front of the coach. Taking hold of the door, Godric opened it up, waiting for the screaming to start.

None came.

"My deepest apologies, Miss Parr—" Still no screaming. "Miss Parr?" Godric thrust his head into the coach.

It was empty. Not even a fire-breathing dragon of a chaperone, not that he'd expected one. His sources had assured him she would be alone tonight.

Godric looked over his shoulder. "Ash? You're sure this is Parr's coach?"

"Of course. Why?" Ashton jumped off his horse, marched over and thrust his head into the empty coach. He was silent a long moment before he withdrew. Ashton put his finger against his lips and motioned to the inside. A tuft of pink muslin peeped out from the wooden seat. He gestured for Godric to step away from the coach.

Ashton lowered his voice. "It seems that our little rabbit chase has turned into a fox hunt. She's hidden in the hollow space of the seat, clever girl."

"Hiding under the seat?" Godric shook his head, bewildered. He didn't know one woman of his acquaintance who would do something so clever.

Perhaps Evangeline, but then if anything could be said of that woman, it was that she was far from ordinary. A prickling of excitement coursed through his veins, into his chest. He loved a challenge.

"Let's wait a few minutes and see if she emerges."

Godric looked back at the coach, impatience prickling inside him. "I don't want to wait here all night."

"She'll come out soon enough. Allow me." Ashton walked back to the coach and called out to Godric in a carrying voice. "Blast and damnation! She must have slipped out before we took charge of the coach. Just leave it. We'll take the driver back to London tomorrow." Ashton shut the door with a loud slam and motioned for Godric to join him.

"Now we wait," Ashton whispered. He indicated that he would guard the left coach door while Godric stationed himself at the right.

Emily listened to the drum of retreating hooves and silently counted to one hundred. Her heart jolted in her chest as she considered what the men would do if they caught her. Highwaymen could be cruel and murderous, especially if their quarry offered little. She had no access to her father's fortune, which left only her body.

Icy dread gripped Emily's spine, paralyzing her limbs. She drew a breath as anxiety spiraled through her.

I must be brave. Fight them until I can fight no more. With trembling hands, she pushed at the roof of the seat, wincing as it popped open. Once she climbed out, she brushed dirt from her gown, noticing some tears from the rough wood on the inside of the seat. But the tears held no importance. All that mattered was survival.

Emily looked out the coach window. Nothing stood out in the darkness. Only the faint glimmer of moonlight touched the road with milky tendrils. Stars winked and flickered overhead, pale lights, distant and cold. A shudder wracked her frame, and Emily hugged herself, wanting so much to be at home. She missed her warm bed and her parents' murmurs from down the hall. It was a comfort she'd taken for granted. But she couldn't afford to think about them, not when she was in danger.

Were the men truly gone? Could it really be this easy?

She opened the coach door, and stepped down onto the dirt road. Strong arms locked about her waist and yanked her backward. The collision with a hard body knocked the breath from her lungs. Terror spiked her blood as she struggled against the arms that held her.

"Good evening, my darling," a low voice murmured.

Emily screamed once, before she bit down on the hand that covered her mouth. She tasted the smooth leather of fine riding gloves.

The man roared and nearly dropped her. "Damn!"

Emily rammed an elbow backwards into her attacker's stomach and began to wrestle free until he grabbed her arm. She swung about, striking him across the face with a balled fist. The man staggered back, leaving her free to dive inside the coach.

If she could get to the other side and run, she might stand a chance. She scrabbled towards the door, but never made it. The devil surged into the coach after her. Turning to face him, she was knocked flat onto her back.

She screamed again as his body settled over hers.

The dim moonlight revealed his bright eyes and strong features.

He caught her flailing wrists, pinning them above her head. "Quiet!"

Emily wanted to rake his eyes out, but the man was relentless. His hips ground against hers and panic drove her to a new level of terror. Her fears of being forcibly taken surfaced as his warm breath fanned over her face and neck. She shrieked, and he reared back away from her, as though the sound confused him.

"I'm not going to hurt you." His voice vibrated with a low growl, ruining any promise his words might carry.

"You're hurting me now!" She yanked her arms uselessly against his hold.

The man eased off her somewhat, and Emily took her chance. She tucked her knees up, and with all the power she could summon, she kicked. Her attacker stumbled out the open door and fell onto his back. Emily barely registered that he was winded before she turned and exited the other side of the coach.

The moment she emerged, another man lunged for her. To escape him, Emily fell back against the side of the coach. Rather than grab her, he held his arms wide to keep her from slipping by him, like he was corralling livestock.

"Easy, easy," he purred.

Emily whipped her head to the left and pleaded with her mind to think, but the man she'd bitten rounded the corner and pounced, pinning her against the coach, his arms caging her in. His solid muscular body towered over her. His jaw clenched as though one move from her would trigger something dark and wild. Emily's breath caught, and her heart pounded violently against her ribs.

The man was panting and angry. The intensity of his eyes mesmerized her, but the second he blinked, the spell broke and she fought with every bit of strength she could muster.

The Story continues in *Wicked Designs*, The League of Rogues Book 1 available wherever books are sold.

Want to read the first chapter of the sensual love story *Tempted By A Rogue*? Please turn the page to read about how Gemma falls for her childhood sweetheart's best friend, the brooding naval officer Jasper Holland.

Midhurst, West Sussex 1817

White and pink roses formed spots of striking color against the dense green hedges as Gemma Haverford walked through the gardens of her home. She let her fingertips touch the petals of the roses as she headed toward the center of the garden. Twilight was her favorite time of day. Birds began to quiet their singing, the sunlight softened, giving everything a soft glow. Gemma took a seat on a cool marble bench at the center of the maze of hedges and rosebushes. Her hands trembled as she smoothed out her skirts. She was anxious enough that her knees knocked together too, but she couldn't banish her nerves.

It wasn't every day that she wore her best gown, an almost sheer sky blue silk, for a secret garden rendezvous. Everything needed to be perfect. She'd gone to great effort to have her lady's maid tame the wild waves of her hair and help to slightly dampen her gown to cling better to her form, which bore only the veiled protection of a single filmy shift.

She had to look her best tonight. At twenty-five she was past the age where most women found it easy to marry. One of her distant cousins had callously remarked earlier that year that she was so far back on the shelf that she was collecting dust. Gemma, feeling a little too irritated at the remark, and having one too many cups of arrack punch, had sneezed at him as though he was the one covered in dust. Not her finest moment, she had nearly dissolved in a fit of unladylike giggles at his horrified expression when he'd struggled to find the handkerchief in his waistcoat to wipe his face.

There was a very good reason she hadn't married, but she couldn't tell anyone, not even her parents why she'd turned down more than one suitor over the years. For eleven years she had kept herself out of the hunt for husbands, believing, *knowing* that she would marry one man, James Randolph, her childhood sweetheart.

He and his best friend, Jasper Holland, had enlisted in His Majesty's Navy as young midshipman. James had been fourteen and Jasper, half a year older, had been fifteen. For eleven long years the two men had been gone, making their fortunes on the high seas, but now they set to return home, to marry and settle down. She'd not seen them in all that time, but she knew in her heart of hearts, that James was coming for her. His letters to her had been steady and filled with reassurances of his affection and his intent to marry her as soon as he came home. And now it was time.

What would he be like after so many years? Had he changed like she had? Grown taller, more muscular, more handsome than the wild young man who'd dashed off to sea? Would he be stern as a husband after commanding men and war ships? Or would he be gentle with her after so many hard years at sea, and want nothing more than a quiet country life full of friends and family within an easy walk of one's home? It was what she'd always wanted. She'd never cared for London and the fast pace of the city. She adored the country, the birds, the green lands, the sheep, even the garden parties that her neighbors threw often were an amusement she enjoyed. Would James want the same thing?

Gemma nibbled her bottom lip, glancing about the gardens. Wisteria hung over trellises to the entrance of this particular part of the garden, the thick blooms almost like wildflowers strung on green vines over the white painted wood. How lovely it was here tonight. How perfect too. She couldn't resist smiling.

Just that morning she had received James's latest letter, telling her he would seek her out in the gardens tonight, for a private audience, away from the eyes of parents and chaperones.

Tonight. The one word held such promise. Enclosed in James's letter was a soft strip of black gauzy cloth embroidered with silver stars. The letter instructed her to wait until twilight, and then blindfold herself for his arrival because he wished to surprise her.

A wave of heat flooded her cheeks at the thought

of being so vulnerable and alone with him in such a manner, but another part of her heated in strange, unfamiliar places. She knew meeting him here like this wasn't proper and if anyone found out, she'd be compromised. But this was James, her James. The man she trusted more than anyone else in the world, except for her father. The temptation to meet him here, even in secret, was irresistible.

What would he do when he came upon her? Remove the blindfold? He might touch her face, her hair, her neck…Gemma trailed her own fingertips over her neck, wondering how different it would feel to have a man's hands there, ones worn with callouses from years of working the ropes while tacking the sails of a great ship.

A shiver rippled through her and she hastily dropped her hands back to her lap, feeling a little foolish. It was so easy to get carried away when thinking of James. When she first read the portion of the letter that told her to meet him like this, being compromised was her first fear, but James was a good and noble man. He was not the sort to ruin a lady, especially not when he intended to marry in good standing.

Even though she had not seen him since he set off eleven years ago, she had faith that he would not damage her virtue with this garden rendezvous. He would be a gentleman, wouldn't he? Gemma was all too aware that she knew little of the hearts of men, or how deeply they could fall prey to their desires.

Perhaps I ought to go back inside and wait for him to call upon me tomorrow morning? That would be the proper thing, after all.

Proper yes, but she wanted to see James alone and didn't want to wait another moment, even one night. If she were to be caught in a position that sorely injured her reputation, well, her father would demand a marriage immediately, James would comply, and all would be well.

Yes, all would be well enough. We need to be married, and mayhap it matters little how the deed comes about?

Perhaps that was what James intended, a certainty of compromising her so he could ensure they would be married. It was indeed a little unorthodox, but that might be his intent. To conquer her like he'd conquered his enemies upon the seas, swiftly and surely. If that were the case, then he was certainly a rogue. Another little smile twisted her lips.

Am I to marry a rogue? Wouldn't that be... She giggled unable to stop herself from thinking of how wonderfully wicked that would be. It would be scandalous, but if it was James, he would be *her* rogue.

So with that reassuring thought, she pulled the blindfold out, carefully put it over her eyes, and tied it into a small bow at the back of her head. She fiddled with her hair, tugging the loose untamable ringlets a little so they coiled down against her neck. Mary, her maid had done her best to fix it, but they both knew it would always look a bit wild. James would have to forgive her for appearing a little unruly. At least her gown had turned out well.

With the blindfold secure, she found she could

see the vague outline of shapes through the thin gauzy cloth but her eyes were, for the most part, shielded from any clearer perceptions. Gemma smoothed her gown again, shifting restlessly as her stomach flipped over and over inside her. What if James had met with some delay, for he was not *officially* due to arrive in Midhurst until tomorrow where he and Jasper would be toasted and celebrated at Lady Edith Greenley's country estate garden party.

Gravel suddenly crunched close by as someone trod along the garden path leading straight toward her. She held her breath, sitting very still. It had to be James. Her heart fluttered so wildly that her ribs hurt from the hammering beat.

Jasper Holland cursed for the thousand time as he fumbled his way through the maze of the Haverford Gardens. It was a bloody mess, this whole situation. It was James who should be here, not him, yet he was the one who was trapped in the situation of compromising a thoroughly decent young lady because his best friend was acting like a cur. Straightening his blue naval coat around his waist, he took another right turn, facing a dead end.

"Who designed this damnable thing? I'll likely lose my way and be eaten by a Minotaur," he muttered, stumbled back and took a left down another path. Someone should have drawn him a map to this—

He heard a feminine giggle some distance away and halted. The sound was light, a little husky, and it had the strangest effect on him just then. He could almost picture a woman beneath him in bed, just as he was about to enter her and ride her to their mutual pleasure making that sound. It was the best sort of sound in the world and one he hadn't heard in a long time. On the sea, there were often chances to visit the docks when in port, and pay for a night at a brothel. James had done that often enough, but Jasper never liked it.

There was something sad about the painted faces and the quiet resigned looks of the prostitutes that betrayed the way they felt about the manner in which they earned their living. More than once Jasper would pay to simply talk to them and then leave for the night, unsatisfied. After that, he'd taken to staying on the ship, leaving James to cavort on his own.

It still amazed him that after all these years he and James were friends. Many men were separated at sea and went years without seeing anyone. Losing touch often resulted in friendships waning. However, that hadn't happened with him and James. They'd been assigned to the same frigate, the *HMS Neptune* as midshipmen after attending a naval college. They'd both been promoted to first lieutenants and by the time they were ready to leave service, they were both still on the same ship.

Due to the influx of men joining the service, the waiting list to be promoted to captain was extensive and neither he nor James had enough peerage connections to curry favor for a quicker rise in officer status. Ergo they'd both agreed the time was good enough to leave service and return home. James had always been a bit of a rakehell, even as a young man before they'd left for the sea, but time had hardened both him and Jasper in different ways. He'd been more hesitant than Jasper to return to Midhurst and even the day before was talking about moving to London once he'd selected a pretty wife, one he could easily tire of and take mistresses later if he so chose. London was much better for mistresses than a little town like Midhurst.

"Love is for fools. Lust is what keeps a man going."

It was something James always said, something he'd taken to believing after so many years at sea. The women in ports had turned James into a jaded man and he'd abandoned dreams of marrying Gemma Haverford, the sweet little country gentleman's daughter he'd left behind.

"Jas, do a man a favor, write Gemma and break it off," he sneered under his breath in imitation of James's plea all those years ago.

It had started out so simple. A favor for a friend.

"And I'm the fool who took over writing those bloody love letters," Jasper growled in self-directed frustration.

He'd written one letter to Gemma, doing his best to imitate James's poor handwriting, but the words to end things…well they just hadn't come out on the page. Instead he found himself sharing details of his day, thoughts and impressions he had of the islands they'd visited, the strange lands and natives they'd encountered, the battles they'd faced. His fears, his hopes, his own dreams. And he'd signed that first letter with a single letter J. Not as James, but Jasper, the man he was. He hadn't wanted to deceive her any more than he had to. Her response to his first letter had been almost immediate. A letter back to him found him so quickly through the post that he had to assume she'd written it the second she'd received his letter.

The Gemma he'd met through her letters had fascinated him, amused him, and changed the way he thought of Midhurst. The little girl with ginger hair had changed so much. She'd become a woman worth knowing. Her stories and descriptions of the town, the village, the countryside, everything that was so easy to forget at sea, had kept him grounded and reminded him of home. It was no longer a place he'd escaped from to live a life of adventure, but become a wonderful place of refuge for him, a sanctuary to someday return to when his service was over.

But the game was now at an end.

James had found out on their last week aboard ship that Jasper hadn't broken off the secret engagement and that he'd continued to write to Gemma for the last ten years. James had been furious to learn that Gemma was now fully under the impression James was going to propose to her and that she'd saved herself for him and him alone. Jasper had read every letter where she'd detailed the passing London Seasons and how she'd felt a little pressured to marry, but had insisted she loved him and would wait. For James. Not him. The thought summoned a black cloud over Jasper's thoughts, but it wasn't going to change what he had to do tonight. He had to end it with Gemma while pretending to be James. Compromise her so that tomorrow morning when she met with James, he could discover she'd kissed another man and break it off with her forever.

Yes, it would ruin her, but Jasper had every intent of making things right, of marrying her himself. He would just have to convince her of that once the dust settled from James crying off. Jasper could wait, *would* wait for as long as he had to for Gemma to be his wife, his lover, his world. His only fear was that she would despise him for his deception all these years, but it was a risk he would have to take. He'd led her to believe he would marry her in his letters and he'd meant every word. If only he hadn't hidden behind the facade of being James.

I should have confessed my identity from the start, before I wove this tangled web, but 'tis too late now.

A bitter taste coated his tongue. Scowling, he peered through the nearest bush. He could just make out a feminine figure seated on a bench. It was a sight he'd never forget. The woman was lovely. She had a full figure, hips just the right size for a man's hands, and the perfect indent of a narrow waist. From where he stood, he couldn't see her front, but the twilight highlighted the riotous ginger colored waves of her hair that were escaping the nest of pins atop her head. She looked like a delicious little minx ready for a tumble into the nearest bed.

Lord, he wanted to be the man to take her to

bed, to explore Gemma in a way he'd only fantasized about for years. Of course that had been purely dreams, he hadn't thought she'd look so tempting in real life. He remembered the little ginger-haired girl that had followed him and James about when they were children. He'd never had much interest in girls, but James had rather enjoyed the way she'd gazed at him with those sweet calf eyes. Adoration, no matter where the source came from had always been something James enjoyed and it had been only too easy for him to woo little Gemma with his smiles and teasing. Jasper had been far too busy to deal with girls at that age, he'd been more interested in exploring the hills and forests of Midhurst and getting in the sort of trouble boys were prone to do.

The woman on the bench sighed touched the blindfold over her eyes. It was made from a strip of cloth he'd found just for her in a little shop in a seaside port only a week ago. It was to be his tool of deception, a way to keep her from seeing him clearly, so she'd look back upon tonight and have to admit it was not James who'd visited her. It was a cruel plan. James's plan, not his, but Jasper was equally a bastard for going along with it.

"Hellfire and damnation," he muttered, squared his shoulders and walked around the nearest hedge. The time to compromise an innocent lady had arrived and he couldn't put it off another moment.

Forgive me, sweet Gemma.

ACKNOWLEDGMENTS

As always, there are so many people for an author to thank and it's difficult to list everyone. My biggest thanks are to my readers and fans who take a chance on my books and those who contact me to let me know they enjoy the books. I also have to thank Nadia and Rohit, my dear friends from my early writing days while in law school. They read Gareth and Helen's story first in its rough format and they helped guide me in the art of writing as I was just beginning to write romance.